A BLUE KNIGHT TO REMEMBER

LEONARD VARASANO

www.dizzyemupublishing.com

DIZZY EMU PUBLISHING
1714 N McCadden Place, Hollywood, Los Angeles 90028
www.dizzyemupublishing.com

A Blue Knight To Remember
Leonard Varasano

ISBN: 9798705212682

First published in the United States
in 2021 by Dizzy Emu Publishing

www.dizzyemupublishing.com

A BLUE KNIGHT TO REMEMBER

LEONARD VARASANO

A Blue Knight to Remember

Screenplay

by

Leonard Varasano

FADE IN:

The Heart of a Good Man is the Sanctuary
of God in this World

Suzanne Curchod

The radiant letters composing the passage slowly
intensifies brighter and brighter, accompanied by an
angelic resonance increasing in tandem with the display of
light.

FADE TO BLACK

FADE IN FROM BLACK

INT. HOSPITAL CORRIDOR

A visibly distraught woman, ISABELLA, is standing face to
face with a clipboard-toting doctor outside the opened door
of an intensive-care room in a bustling, sepia-toned
hospital corridor. She keeps glancing from the doctor to
the room, clearly distracted.

> DOCTOR
> We've done all we could...He's in
> God's hands now.

The woman lowers her head. For a moment she seems to give
in, her resolve crumbling, when suddenly she looks at the
doctor, chin up, defiance in her eyes.

> ISABELLA
> The drugs you gave him will work only
> if I'm by his side...In all my years
> of nursing I've earned that love is
> the strongest medicine of all.

As the doctor slowly nods his head, the woman turns and
enters the hospital room.

FADE TO:

INT. HOSPITAL ROOM - NIGHT

Deeps shadows accentuate a dimly lit hospital room, veiling
Isabella sitting beside a small boy on the bed. The boy,
CHRIS SIMONE, her son, is covered in a feverish sweat,
shivering violently, thrashing his head side to side on his
drenched pillow. Isabella dips a washcloth in an ice water
filled basin, wrings slightly then gently applies it to the
boy's forehead.

EXTREME CLOSEUP: CHRIS' FACE

Chris' eyes flutter open, disoriented, pained, though
seemingly focused on something beyond the scope of the
room.

EXT. DARKENED ABYSS - CHRIS' DELIRIUM NIGHTMARE

The boy's fevered dream streaks fast and furious through a
VORTEX of shadowy, writhing figures shrieking through
darkening mists. The movements and screeching of
the ghastly apparitions intensify with the passing of the
moments. Suddenly, an all-encompassing shadowy appendage
reaches to engulf him.

INT. HOSPITAL ROOM - NIGHT

Chris begins thrashing more, terrified with the finality of
his nightmare's embrace. His mother tries to hold him down.
Frantically, tearfully, she looks skyward.

                    ISABELLA
          Please Heavenly Father...please God
          ...help my son!

EXT. DARKENED ABYSS - CHRIS' DELIRIUM NIGHTMARE

Suddenly, a glimmer of light shines from far beyond.
Distant at first, yet true enough to reveal the veracity of
the adage: All the darkness in the world cannot extinguish
the light of a single candle. As the radiance pierces the
gloom, the shadowy figures hastily retreat to obscurity.

                                        (CONTINUED)

CONTINUED:

The light intensifies and in the midst of it all a new
figure appears: a beautiful, alluring woman, with
shimmering hair of gold, eyes blue as the Nordic sky at
sunset, skin fair and smooth as porcelain. Smiling,
dazzling, she reaches towards Chris, kissing his forehead.
The woman is Chris' feverish visualization of an ANGEL.

EXT. GLEAMING OMNIPOTENT RADIANCE

                         ANGEL
                       (whisper)
            Everything is all right now, Chris.

By the look on Chris' face he deeply loves the angel. He
watches, enamored, until the angel unfurls transcendent
wings to begin her heavenly ascent.

                         CHRIS
                (reaches out with his arms)
             Please...I want to stay with you!

                         ANGEL
         (smiling-kissing Chris' forehead once more)
             You have much to do...little one...before
             we shall meet again.

The angel quickly ascends into the aura of light.

                                              FADE TO:

INT. CLOSEUP - CHRIS' FACE

Chris' eyes blink open, this time knowingly, as he looks up

                         CHRIS
                        Momma?

INT. HOSPITAL ROOM - NIGHT

Chris' mother kisses him, her lips pausing on the small
forehead.

                                           (CONTINUED)

CONTINUED:

                    ISABELLA
          Your fever broke...Thank God!

                     CHRIS
          Momma...ho visto un angelo...I saw an
          Angel...she kissed me.

                    ISABELLA
          Sei...il mio angelo...You're my angel!

Mother and son lovingly embrace.

INT. CLOSEUP - CHRIS' FACE

As he hugs his mother, Chris' eyes wander skyward, a look
of wonder on his face.

                 NARRATING VOICE (V.O.)
          Chris envisioned the angelic beauty
          Which had just befallen his eyes, a
          sight surely to transfix his heart
          for the rest of his earthly days.

                                        FADE TO BLACK

FADE IN FROM BLACK

EXT. LITTLE LEAGUE BASEBALL GAME - DAY

A young Chris is at bat during a Little League game. All
his teammates and the fans are yelling with all the
appearances of the game being on the line. Chris swings
hard twice, failing to make contact. He then takes two
pitches which are outside the strike zone. Through the din
Chris hears his father ARTURO'S voice.

EXT. LITTLE LEAGUE GAME - CLOSEUP OF ARTURO

Arturo cups his hands to his mouth and directs his voice to
Chris.

                     ARTURO
          Good eye Chris...good eye! Wait for
          your pitch buddy...wait for *your* pitch!

EXT. LITTLE LEAGUE GAME - CLOSEUP OF CHRIS

Chris nods slightly in response to his father's voice. He
digs his feet in and his expression is absolutely
tenacious.

EXT. LITTLE LEAGUE GAME - DAY

The pitcher delivers the pitch and Chris is ready. He
swings and smashes the ball over the center field fence,
winning the game with a walk off home run. He is swarmed by
his teammates after he crosses home plate, and his father
is waiting there, hoisting him upon his shoulder in
celebratory fashion as Chris smiles skyward.

EXT. FROZEN LAKE - DAYLIGHT

Chris is still a youngster learning how to ice skate with
his father. The pair has the small lake to themselves,
laughing and obviously enjoying one another's company.
Beyond the pond, snow covers the ground and trees as far as
the eye can see.

                                              FADE TO BLACK

FADE IN FROM BLACK

INT. GYMNASIUM - WRESTLING MATCH

Chris the teenager nervously paces as he awaits his match.
There are several mats with matches in progress indicating
a high school tournament setting. COACH AMATO approaches.

                    COACH AMATO
              Win this and you're in the finals.
              You should've beaten this guy last
              time...but this time he's yours.

They glance across the mat at the husky opponent.

                    CHRIS
                  (resolute)
              This time he's mine.

                                              (CONTINUED)

CONTINUED:

                         P.A. ANNOUNCER (V.O.)
                    Now wrestling on mat number three...
                    Martone...Middletown versus Simone...
                    Long Branch.

The largely partisan Middletown crowd chants Martone's name
in unison while stamping their feet into the bleachers.

                         MIDDLETOWN CROWD
                    MAR-TONE! MAR-TONE! MAR-TONE!

Chris turns and sees his father, who gives him a
simultaneous nod, wink and thumbs up sign. Chris nods back
as Coach Amato taps him on his headgear.

                         COACH AMATO
                    Now get him!

Chris goes to the center circle and eyes his opponent. The
referee has the wrestlers shake hands and blows his whistle
to start the match. Chris moves in fast, hitting a double
leg takedown and taking his opponent right to his back. The
other wrestler tries to fight off the pin but Chris grits
his teeth and clamps hard. The referee slaps the mat and
the stunned crowd is silent save for Chris' father, Coach
Amato and a small contingent from Long Branch. Chris is
ecstatic as the referee raises his hand in victory. He
trots off the mat and his coach vigorously shakes his hand.

                         COACH AMATO
                    That's what I call a pin!

Chris sees his father standing near the bleachers and walks
over to him. Arturo is beaming with pride as the two
embrace.

                         ARTURO
                    Way to go, son!

                         CHRIS
                    Thanks, Pop. That one's for you!

                                             FADE TO BLACK

FADE IN FROM BLACK

EXT. POLICE ACADEMY GROUNDS - DAY

A contingent of police recruits dressed in khaki's march sharply to the cadence ushered by a uniformed drill instructor. He guides them throughout the grounds in precise military formation. The group repeats each line of the drill instructor's utterance.

                    DRILL INSTRUCTOR
          Blue Knight Po-lice Academy
          The land that God forgot
          The sand is fourteen inches deep
          The sun is blazing hot
          And we must all remember
          Indeed and we shall tell
          Another Blue Knight reporting sir
          I've served my time in hell

The group marches off into the distance.

EXT. POLICE ACADEMY GROUNDS

The police recruits are on lunch break, relaxing in the tree shade, shooting the breeze near a PT obstacle course. Chris Simone munches on a sandwich when another recruit saunters over with a mischievous, smirky look. His name is BOB ROMANO.

                    BOB ROMANO
          So Simone...you were some sort
          of hot shot wrestling champ?

Chris glances up with that 'you again?' look.

                    CHRIS
          I wouldn't say 'hot shot'.

                    BOB ROMANO
          Self Defense is next week.
          We'll see what you're made of.

(CONTINUED)

CONTINUED:

The recruits within earshot seem to have heard this before
and appear to be enjoying the bravado.

> CHRIS
> You outweigh me by fifty pounds...
> at least.

> BOB ROMANO
> That's right. Think you can handle it?

> CHRIS
> I'm just thinking how embarrassed you'll
> be when I kick your butt.

The other recruits sound off collectively "uh-oh" and "here
we go!"

> BOB ROMANO
> We will see...won't we?

> CHRIS
> Just to make it fair...I'll even
> offer you a handicap.

> BOB ROMANO
> Oh yeah? What handicap?

> CHRIS
> I'll start from the bottom position...
> not that'll help you much.

> BOB ROMANO
> We'll see Simone...we'll see.

INT. POLICE ACADEMY GYMNASIUM

Most of the floor is covered by wrestling mats as the
recruits are paired-off practicing various self-defense
holds, throws and strikes. Instructors offer guidance and
expertise to the recruits. There's lots of panting,
grunting and pained expressions. After several moments, the
head instructor blows a whistle and signals for everyone to
circle around the center mat.

                    HEAD INSTRUCTOR
          Men...what you learn here may very well
          save your life one day. The streets are
          EXTREMELY unforgiving and NOT the place to
          sharpen your skills. Remember what you
          were taught, be vigilant, stay in shape
          and be prepared for that fight to the death
          that statistically...at least one of you
          will encounter with the need to use deadly
          force. If someone uses his hands against you
          then you use your stick...if he uses a
          knife then you use your service weapon and
          cancel his ticket permanently then and
          there. As police officer's you must always
          go home alive and unhurt...put that at the
          top of your daily priority list.

The instructor pauses and eyes the somber faces of the
recruits allowing his words his words to sink in for a few
moments.

                    HEAD INSTRUCTOR
          On a bit of a lighter note I understand
          a wrestling challenge has been issued
          amongst your ranks...Simone...Romano...
          front and center!

The class atmosphere lightens considerably in anticipation
of the matchup brewing for weeks as the two recruits
approach the center of the mat. The size difference between
the pair is readily apparent as Chris is half a head
shorter and considerably lighter than the stocky Romano.

                                              (CONTINUED)

CONTINUED:

                    HEAD INSTRUCTOR
          Are you two ready?

                    ROMANO
          You said you'd take bottom...remember?

                    CHRIS
          I remember.

Chris drops down into the defensive start position. Romano
assumes the top position. The size differential grows even
more apparent.

                    HEAD INSRUCTOR
          Ready...Wrestle!

Chris explodes out of the bottom position before Romano can
react, does a side step and shrug and Romano falls to his
stomach. Chris is now on Romano's back. Romano tries to
counter but Chris quickly bars his arms and flips Romano to
his back. Chris finishes off the move by using his legs to
figure-four Romano's head. Romano is pinned in embarrassing
fashion and the head instructor slaps the mat to signify
match over. The whole display took 10 seconds and the other
recruits burst out in vociferous acclamation. Chris
releases Romano and stands up. The head instructor raises
his hand in victory.

Chris offers his hand to Romano and helps him to his feet.
Romano claps him on the shoulder.

                    ROMANO
               (sheepish)
          Talk about a beatdown...

                    HEAD INSTRUCTOR
               (gesturing towards Chris)
          It's obvious if this fella gets
          his hands on you you're going to
          have problems. Add your service

                                             (CONTINUED)

CONTINUED:

> weapon to the mix and it's not difficult
> to imagine the consequences of losing
> physical control of a situation.
> Never forget what you saw here today
> and NEVER underestimate your opponent
> ...your life and the lives of brother
> officers and innocent people will
> depend on it!

                                        FADE TO BLACK

FADE IN FROM BLACK

INT.   POLICE ACADEMY GRADUATION CEREMONY

In front of a standing room only crowd a uniformed police
bugler marches front and center and plays a sharp rendition
of 'To the Colors'. From the back of the room a large
contingent of uniformed police recruits march in step to
the front of the large room before the stage and remain
standing at attention before the American flag. The police
academy commandant, a distinguished looking man administers
the oath of duty.

                    POLICE COMMANDANT
           Officers at attention, raise your right
           hands and repeat after me: On my honor,
           I will never betray my badge, my integrity,
           my character, nor the public trust. I will
           always have the courage to hold myself
           accountable for my actions. I will always
           uphold the United States Constitution, my
           community and the agency I serve. I will
           constantly strive to achieve those objectives
           and ideals, dedicating myself before God to my
           calling as a Police Officer.

                                        (CONTINUED)

CONTINUED:

The police commandant nods as the police recruits repeat the oath of duty.

                    POLICE COMMANDANT
          Please be seated.

As one the police recruits sit down before the stage, facing the podium.

                    POLICE COMMANDANT
          Congratulations, Men! Today, upon graduation,
          you shall proudly venture forth as the
          stalwart component of our civilized society
          known to all as **police officers**. God-willing,
          your tour of duty for the next 25 years will
          see you through as the guardians and
          protectors of the lives and property of all
          you survey. During your tour, you will emerge
          as the 'go to' person in the lives of the many
          people encountered who, in their time of need,
          require your help, empathy and expertise. If
          you consider this an unappealing prospect and
          if you think of yourself as 'just a cop', then
          your entire career shall never advance beyond
          the limits of your perception.

          Yet, aspire to be a knight, a Blue Knight at
          that, and through your vocation become the one
          who walks tall with honor through the fray,
          in brotherly spirit with the company of
          valiant men so many centuries ago, who once
          swore allegiance to "Protect the weak, the
          defense-less and the helpless while supporting
          the general welfare of all mankind." This
          notion of positive change within the
          innovative concept of law and order allowed
          humanity to emerge from the havoc of the
          medieval Dark Ages and into the light of
          civilization.

                                              CUT TO:

INT. POLICE ACADEMY GRADUATION - CLOSEUP OF RECRUITS

The camera pans on the faces of the recruits one by one,
each man showing varying degrees of interest in the
commandant's speech, until the camera reaches Chris Simone
and remains upon him. He is rapt with complete and utter
attentiveness, nodding with the commandant's words.

                    POLICE COMMANDANT (V.O.)
          The Knight's Code of Chivalry was a moral
          system of ethics which stated all adherents
          should protect others who could not protect
          themselves, such as children, widows and
          elders, and to always respect the honor of
          women.

          Knights were required to tell the truth at
          all times and not only vow to protect the
          weak but also vow to guard the honor of all
          fellow knights.

                                              CUT TO:

INT. - POLICE ACADEMY GRADUATION - COMMANDANT AT PODIUM

                    POLICE COMMANDANT
          When ready to pledge the chivalrous code
          before his liege, a knight would hear these
          words: "In the name of God, of Saint Michael
          and Saint George, I give you the right to
          bear arms, the power to mete justice." The
          liege would lift his sword over the kneeling
          knight then swiftly lower the flat of the
          blade upon the knight's shoulders with three
          strokes in tandem with the declaration, to
          which the knight would respond accordingly:
          "That duty I will solemnly obey as a
          Chivalrous Knight in the Court of Honor."

          The Police Code of Conduct, the oath of duty
          and honor which all of you have pledged
          today has many parallels with the code of
          your predecessors, and as such the honor
          that binds your legacy with theirs is
          ultimately one and the same.

                                         (CONTINUED)

CONTINUED:

                    In conclusion, go forth, Blue Knights of
                    the 14th Basic Recruit Class and allow your
                    gallantry to emerge as you make the world a
                    safer place for us all!

The audience breaks into a rousing applause. The camera
pans in once more upon Chris Simone and the men sitting on
either side of him. Chris applauds harder and louder than
anyone.

EXT. CITY STREET - SUMMER NIGHT

A young Officer Simone walks the beat late at night, long
after all the businesses are closed. He sees someone
walking up the street and moves in that direction to
investigate. As he approaches he sees it is a man tapping
ahead with a walking stick, wearing aviator sunglasses and
a drab military field jacket, proceeding slowly along. The
man's name is TOM BURKE.

                         CHRIS
                Good evening, Sir.

                         TOM
                   (turning to face Chris)
                Good evening to you, Officer.

                         CHRIS
                   (surprised)
                How did you know I'm a police officer?

                         TOM
                   (grinning)
                Well...you were polite enough to call
                me 'sir'...plus...as you walk...I could
                hear your nightstick moving slightly in
                its holder.

                                        (CONTINUED)

CONTINUED:

                         CHRIS
                    (impressed)
               You can hear that, huh?

                         TOM
               God saw fit to help me along after
               I lost my sight.

                         CHRIS
               You used to see?

                         TOM
               Yeah...until Nam...but I can't
               complain...at least I came home.

The expression on Chris' face shows he is moved by Tom's
faith and patriotism.

                         CHRIS
               So you walk at night to avoid traffic?

                         TOM
               Well...sure...but it's always nighttime
               to me, sonny.

Chris chuckles.

                         CHRIS
               My name's Chris Simone. It's a pleasure to
               meet you.

                         TOM
               Tom Burke...just call me Tom.

Tom reaches out and Chris shakes his hand.

                         CHRIS
               I'm going to finish making my rounds.
               You take care.

                                             (CONTINUED)

CONTINUED:

As Chris walks away, Tom calls over to him.

                        TOM
              You take care too.

                                        FADE TO BLACK

FADE IN FROM BLACK

EXT. HIGHWAY - CAR ACCIDENT SCENE - NIGHT

Officer Chris Simone surveys an accident scene bathed in
the blazing floodlights of his patrol car. A blue Mustang
convertible protrudes from where a station wagon's
passenger compartment used to be, an airborne projectile
which vaulted the highway's concrete divider separating the
north and southbound lanes and had impaled the wagon's roof
like an unexploded missile.

EXT. CITY STREET - POLICE CRUISER - NIGHT

Jumping out of his car Chris hurries towards the wreck
while calling into his portable radio for the first-aid
squad to expedite to the scene. Glass shards crackle under
his boots. His face reflects the dread of the moment about
to greet him.

EXT. ACCIDENT SCENE - NIGHT

Shining his flashlight inside the Mustang, Chris finds many
empty beer cans but no occupant, so he concentrates on
gaining access inside the station wagon below. As he aims
the light through a small opening between the two cars a
muffled moan from within can be heard. Looking inside, he
gasps at the sight illuminated by the beam.

INT. CAR INTERIOR

In the crushed backseat, still wearing seatbelts are two
little children: A little girl in a white-laced dress, and

                                        (CONTINUED)

CONTINUED:

a little boy wearing a dark jacket and tie. Even in the dim
light it is obvious the girl's injury is devastatingly
mortal. The boy seemingly fixes the cop's light with a
vacant stare, glistening tears upon his cheeks.

INT. CLOSEUP OF CHRIS SIMONE'S FACE

Chris does his best to keep an impassive face and not allow
the horror to get the best of him. He manages a reassuring
voice to the boy.

                    CHRIS
          Everything's all right buddy.
          I'll have you out in a minute.

Reaching inside to offer a comforting pat to the boy, he
recoils with a handful of blood, as the child's head falls
down towards his chest; the back of his head gone, sheared
away during the collision.

                    CHRIS
                 (whispers)
          Death tears.

                    WOMAN'S VOICE (O.S. - FRAIL)
          Are my children all right?

Closing his eyes for a moment, Chris takes a deep breath
and backs out of the confines of the crushed backseat.

EXT. ACCIDENT SCENE - NIGHT

Maneuvering around the exterior of the crushed car, he
slides through an opening.

INT. CAR INTERIOR - CRUSHED FRONT SEAT

Chris is met by a mother's pleading, melancholy eyes.

                                        (CONTINUED)

CONTINUED:

                    MOTHER
          Are my children alright?

She speaks with great effort, in obvious shock. Chris
notices the woman is bleeding profusely from a scalp wound
and a ghastly bone shard protrudes from her leg, ripping a
bloody gash through her slacks.

                    CHRIS
          Everything's fine.

                    MOTHER
          Please tell me...they're okay.

The woman grabs Chris' hand.

                    MOTHER
          We...We just came from their spring
          recital.

                    CHRIS
          Everything's fine. Just relax and I'll
          have you out of here soon. What's your
          name?

                    MOTHER
          Mary.

                    CHRIS
          Mary, could you give me a phone number?
          I'll call someone at your house the first
          chance I get.

                    MARY
          My husband died last year...I have no one
          ...there's no one to call.

Mary begins to cry. She never gets loud but the tears flow.
In the distance the wail of sirens grows louder.

                                        (CONTINUED)

CONTINUED:

                    MARY
          I can't feel my legs!

                    CHRIS
          That's normal...lots of people can't
          after an accident. Try to relax.

                    MARY
            (looking at her hands)
          My head hurts...where's all this blood
          from?

                    CHRIS
          You have a little cut. It's okay though
          ...scalp wounds always look worse than
          they are.

Mary's eyes suddenly dart to Chris' impassive face.

                    MARY (wailing)
          How come I can't hear my children?
          Michelle...Johnny...answer me...
          ANSWER ME!

INT. CAR - CLOSEUP OF MARY and CHRIS' HANDS

Mary digs her nails into Chris' wrist.

INT. CAR - CLOSEUP OF CHRIS' FACE

Chris is distraught but he hides it well. His eyes wander.

INT. CAR - MANGLED REAR VIEW MIRROR

Highlighted by the aura of Chris' flashlight, a hand carved
olivewood crucifix hangs twisted from the mirror, the
tortured visage of Christ staring forever heavenward.

INT. CAR

Chris quickly averts his eyes from the crucifix. He glances
backwards as a gloved hand protruding from a yellow
windbreaker sleeve taps him on the shoulder. He gently
peels Mary's grip on his wrist but then takes hold of her
hand.

                    CHRIS
                  (softly)
          Mary...the paramedics are here...
          they're going to help you now.

                    MARY
                  (sobbing)
          Please...don't leave me...please!

                    CHRIS
          I'll be right outside...there's only
          room for one person in here.

                    MARY
          Make sure they help my babies...
          Please Officer!

                    CHRIS
          I will Mary...I will.

EXT. ACCIDENT SCENE - NIGHT

Chris backs out of the car and faces the paramedic.

                    CHRIS
                  (whispering)
            The children...in the backseat...
            they're dead. The mom...she's in
            bad shape...don't tell her...not
            yet anyway.

The paramedic opens his mouth to protest but says nothing
after noting Chris' grim expression. Chris spins away. The
highway is now swarming with emergency personnel, flashing
lights and morbid onlookers. Another patrolman approaches
Chris to inquire about the accident but Chris abruptly
waves him off while making a beeline for his patrol car. He
opens the door and enters.

INT. POLICE CAR

Chris punches the dashboard once...twice...three times with all his strength, then lowers his head into his hands. A tap on the window brings him around. Looking up he sees the other cop standing there eyeing him with great concern.

Chris opens the door.

                    COP
          You okay, Brother?

Chris wipes his wet eyes on his uniform sleeve.

                    CHRIS
          Yeah...no problem.

                    COP
          The driver of the Mustang's
          over there.

The cop points across the highway.

EXT. HIGHWAY - ADJACENT TO ACCIDENT SCENE - NIGHT

Sitting on the curb away from the onlookers a YOUNG MAN sits with one arm dangling over his knees while the other hand supports his head. He is engrossed in watching the rescuers setup the extrication equipment.

EXT. HIGHWAY NEAR PATROL CAR - NIGHT

The officers walk towards the young man sitting on the curb. The man notices them approaching and stands with slow and profound unsteadiness. The cops draw within an arm's length of the man and study him with intensity. The man is clearly uninjured and returns the police scrutiny with an impish smirk.

                    CHRIS
          Were you driving the Mustang?

                    YOUNG MAN
          Yessir, Officer.

(CONTINUED)

CONTINUED:

Leering, the man wobbles as he lurches forward, mocking
Chris with a left-handed salute designed solely to
antagonize the recipient.

EXT. CLOSEUP OF CHRIS' HANDS

Chris' hands slowly ball into white knuckled fists. After a
long moment, he slowly opens his hands.

EXT. HIGHWAY - NIGHT

                    CHRIS
          You're under arrest.

Chris spins the young man around, pats him down, handcuffs
him and then walks him to the patrol car. Opening the rear
door he guides him to the backseat before slamming the door
shut. Chris turns and faces the other cop.

                    CHRIS
          It's going to be a long night.

The other cop glances through the patrol car rear window
and turns to Chris.

                    COP
          Rest assured he'll be a prison punk.

Nodding, Chris enters the patrol car and slowly drives off.

                                        FADE TO BLACK

FADE IN FROM BLACK

EXT. ROADWAY ADJACENT TO RED BRICK CHURCH - DAY

As the sun rises a sedan stops in the driveway next to ST.
MICHAEL'S CHURCH. Chris emerges wearing street clothes. His
face is grim and he appears exhausted. Slowly he mounts the
steps, pulls open one of the two large doors and enters the
church.

INT. CHURCH

Chris proceeds towards the front of the empty church. He
genuflects in the aisle then kneels in the front pew,
lowering his head in prayer.

INT. CHURCH - RECTORY ENTRANCE

A priest cracks open the rectory door and peers into the
church. FATHER ARMAND sees Chris kneeling in prayer. He
closes the door without sound.

INT.CHURCH

Chris stands and walks to the rectory door. He knocks
softly. A moment later Father Armand opens the door. He
smiles but sees Chris' distraught face and turns serious.

                    FATHER ARMAND
          Good morning, Chris...is everything
          all right?

                    CHRIS
          No Father...I was hoping to make a
          confession this morning.

                    FATHER ARMAND
          Sure Chris. I'll be there in a moment.

INT. CHURCH CONFESSIONAL BOOTH

Chris sits pensively in his side of the confessional. The
partition opens and Father Armando's silhouette can be seen
through the translucent partition screen. Chris makes the
sign of the cross.

                    CHRIS
           Bless me Father for I have sinned.
          it's been one month since my last
          confession.

                    FATHER ARMAND
          What is the sin you wish to confess,
          my son?

(CONTINUED)

CONTINUED:

                    CHRIS
          Last night I lied, Father. I lied
          during the course of my police duties.

                    FATHER ARMAND
          What were the circumstances?

                    CHRIS
               (voice cracking)
          Bad accident...I was the first responder...
          found two little kids dead in the backseat...
          their mother alive in the front seat...she
          was in real bad shape...she asked me about
          her children...she was in shock from her
          injuries and I didn't want to risk killing
          her...I lied to her...told her everything's
          okay.

Tears stream down Chris' cheeks.

                    FATHER ARMAND
          Is there anything else?

                    CHRIS
          No, Father.

                    FATHER ARMAND
          Well...I believe God knows your good
          intention. Your sin is truly forgiven.
          Go in peace.

                    CHRIS
          Thanks be to God...Thank you, Father.

Chris again makes the sign of the cross then stands and
exits the booth.

                                        FADE TO BLACK

FADE IN FROM BLACK

INT. POLICE DEPARTMENT BRIEFING ROOM

Chris is the first one present for roll call and the daily
briefing. Soon two other officers enter the room. Chris is
reading wanted posters when SERGEANT ADDISON walks into the
room.

                    SERGEANT ADDISON
          Simone...good to see you're at
          least punctual.

Chris nods and smiles.

                    SERGEANT ADDISON
          Looks like you got some color...
          isn't this the time of year you
          guineas start turning dark?

Chris loses his smile as Sgt. Addison starts giggling as if
what he had just said was the funniest thing ever. When he
sees Chris is not laughing he turns snide.

                    SERGEANT ADDISON
          What's the matter...can't take a joke?

                    CHRIS
          Sure...I can take a joke...if it's funny.

The two men glare at one another. Chris turns and walks out
of the room.

                                        FADE TO BLACK

FADE IN FROM BLACK

INT. APARTMENT LIVING ROOM WINDOW - DAY

Blizzard conditions exist beyond the view from the interior
of a living room window. As the camera pans below the
window Chris and another uniformed police officer are
offering comfort to a distressed pregnant woman while

                                        (CONTINUED)

CONTINUED:

delivering her baby as the storm rages on. The women's name
is LAVANYA and the officer's name is JOE O'CONNOR.

                    CHRIS
          Baby's almost here.

                    LAVANYA
          Hurts so much...Hurts so much...HURTS SO
          MUCH.

                    CHRIS
          Nice...deep...breaths.

Chris makes eye contact with Lavayna. He pants to encourage
her to do the same which she does for a few moments.

                    LAVANYA
          Oh God...where's the ambulance?

                    JOE O'CONNOR
          The blizzard's causing all sorts
          of delays. I think your baby's
          going to be here first.

                    LAVANYA
          Sweet Jesus...Sweet Jesus...Sweet
          JE-SUS...aaahhhh!

There's a moment of silence before the newborn baby's cries
sound forth, eliciting wide smiles from Chris and Joe. The
baby is placed in a swaddling blanket.

                    CHRIS
          You have a baby girl, Lavanya!

Chris places the swaddled baby in her mother's arms as
Lavayna weeps tears of joy at the new life she now holds.

                                        FADE TO BLACK

FADE IN FROM BLACK

INT. DINING ROOM. DAY

Chris sits at the dining table eating dinner with his
mother Isabella and father Arturo. Chris seems despondent,
and his parents take turns looking at him and then one
another. Even with Frank Sinatra playing on the stereo the
atmosphere is heavy. Finally, Isabella speaks.

                    ISABELLA
          So Chris...what's new with Long Branch's
          finest officer?

                    CHRIS
          (shrugs)
          Nothing much. Some days are better than
          others...like a couple weeks ago, I helped
          deliver a baby.

                    ISABELLA
          That's wonderful! Boy or girl?

                    CHRIS
          A baby girl.

Chris smiles at his mother but then lowers his eyes to his
plate. Isabella and Arturo exchange concerned glances.

                    ARTURO
          You know...you can always talk to your
          mom or me...about anything.

                    CHRIS
          I know, Pop. I appreciate that...
          really do. It's just...there's some
          things...it's best to put behind me.

Chris smiles at his parents but it's obvious he has much on
his mind. Arturo reaches and taps Chris twice on the
forearm.

                    ISABELLA
          How about some coffee?

(CONTINUED)

CONTINUED:

Chris and Arturo both nod yes.

INT. POLICE LOCKER ROOM

Chris walks towards his locker as other officers stand
close by, eyeing him. He doesn't notice being watched and
opens the locker door when suddenly an enraged male mallard
duck bursts out with flapping wings, quacking away madly,
attacking the first thing it could see which is Chris, who
nearly falls over backwards with the shock of the fowl's
assault. The other officers present quickly double over,
laughing hysterically as Chris fends off the duck, finally
grabbing hold behind its head with one hand and restraining
the surprisingly strong wings with his other arm. With
hasty motivation Chris makes his way to the nearby back exit
and turns the creature loose, which soon finds its balance
and flies away.

Chris returns to his locker and the other cops are still
laughing.

                    CHRIS
          Not very funny, fellas.

Chris' deadpan, matter of fact response makes the men whoop
harder still.

INT. PATROL CAR - DAY

Chris is parked in his patrol cruiser in the parking lot of
St. Michael's Church, engrossed in writing a report. It's
drizzling outside and the windshield wipers are set on
delay. Chris turns his head to look outside his window as
something catches his eye.

EXT. PATROL CAR - DAY

A female mallard duck is waddling up to his car with a
sense of urgency from the direction of a lake across the
street.

INT.   PATROL CAR - DAY

Chris rolls down his window.

                    CHRIS
          Hey there. Did the fellas send
          you over?

Chuckling, Chris looks around to see if anyone is watching.
The duck responds with a resounding quack. After a second
quack he exits the car.

EXT.   PATROL CAR

Looking around once more, Chris follows as the duck waddles
to the side of the road bordering the lake. The duck stops
at the opening of a storm drain basin collecting rainwater
runoff and quacks again. Chris peers down through the
grating.

INT. STORM DRAIN BASIN

Four ducklings are treading water several feet down.

EXT.   ROADWAY BESIDE STORM DRAIN BASIN

Chris turns toward the mallard hen.

                    CHRIS
          Okay Mom, I'll get them out.

EXT.   CHURCH PARKING LOT

Chris opens the trunk of the police cruiser and removes
makeshift equipment to use in the duckling rescue.

                    CHRIS
          Five-one to headquarters, please
          start an incident card. I'll be
          out of the car near Takanassee
          Lake next to St. Michael's Church.

(CONTINUED)

CONTINUED:

As Chris prepares his makeshift rescue gear, a second
patrol car arrives, driven by Officer Joe O'Connor. He eyes
the duck standing nearby, perplexed.

                    JOE O'CONNOR
          What've we got, Chris?

                    CHRIS
          Somehow, some ducklings washed
          down there.

As Chris gestures down the drain, the mallard hen quacks
again.

Joe O'Connor's eyes grow mischievous.

                    JOE O'CONNOR
          Need a hand?

                    CHRIS
          Sure, I can use a hand.

Joe O'Connor exits his vehicle and looks down the drain,
then gestures toward the mallard hen.

                    JOE O'CONNOR
          Did she wave you down as you
          drove by?

                    CHRIS
          Actually, she came up to me
          when I was parked over there.

Chris motions towards his police cruiser in the church
parking lot.

                    CHRIS
          At first, I thought you were
          setting me up again.

                                        (CONTINUED)

CONTINUED:

Suddenly O'Connor has the expression of someone trying hard
not to burst out laughing.

                    JOE O'CONNOR
          I don't know what you mean.

                    CHRIS
          Really? So you had nothing to do
          with that duck someone stuffed inside
          my locker? You're so full of it!

O'Connor is losing the battle of keeping a straight face.

A car stops on the road adjacent to the church and a young,
pretty woman gets out, camera in hand and approaches the
two officers. Her name is MELISSA WALTERS.

                    MELISSA WALTERS
          Hi there. I'm Melissa Walters from
          the Asbury Park Press. Anything
          worthwhile happening?

She eyes the mallard hen, bewildered.

                    JOE O'CONNOR
          Officer Chris Simone here is about
          to initiate a duck rescue.

The mallard hen quacks again.

                    MELISSA WALTERS
          Oh, I see! Mind if I take some photos?

                    CHRIS
          No, not at all.

                    MELISSA WALTERS
          Thank you!

                                        (CONTINUED)

CONTINUED:

The reporter begins clicking off photo shots. The two
officers resume their task, complicated by the unyielding
position of the drainage grate. The mother duck remains
near, closely monitoring the men.

The ducklings are not cooperative but one by one Chris and
O'Connor snare them and soon the mallard hen is reunited
with her four babies. The feathered family makes their way
to the water's edge and paddle off to the shallows near the
reeds.

                    MELISSA WALTERS
          That was awesome! You guys are great!

She smiles at Chris, clearly interested in him beyond the
duck story.

                    JOE O'CONNOR
          I'll have you know this is not the
          first time Officer Simone has
          facilitated the rescue of waterfowl.

Chris looks at O'Connor in disbelief.

                    MELISSA WALTERS
          It's not?

                    JOE O'CONNOR
          In the recent past, all by himself, he
          extricated a duck that somehow became
          trapped in police headquarters.

                    MELISSA WALTERS
                    (wide-eyed)
          Wow. Is that true?

                    CHRIS
          Well...yes. That's true.

                                        (CONTINUED)

CONTINUED:

                    MELISSA WALTERS
          Would you care to elaborate?
          If not now, maybe another time?

                    CHRIS
          It's really not much of a story.

                    MELISSA WALTERS
          Well, I'd surely like to hear it.

Melissa's blue eyes search Chris' face. There is no doubt
of her interest in him.

                    CHRIS
          Another time would probably be better.

                    MELISSA WALTERS
                      (imploring)
          Here's my card. Please call me?

Melissa Walters returns to her car and looks back at Chris,
smiling. Joe O'Connor waits until she is out of earshot.

                    JOE O'CONNOR
          I hope you follow up with her.
          She's a babe!

                    CHRIS
          She sure is.

Joe O'Connor closely looks at Chris.

                    JOE O'CONNOR
          You do like girls, right?

                    CHRIS
          Sure, I like girls. Why do you ask?

                    JOE O'CONNOR
          Last week, when we all met at the pub

                                        (CONTINUED)

CONTINUED:

                    after work, that Clare Miller tried
                    to show you LOTS of interest, and you
                    had none of it.

                         CHRIS
                    Hey...first of all, she was drunk.
                    Wouldn't be gentlemanly to take
                    advantage. And second, she's been
                    with half the guys on the department.
                    That's not what I'm looking for. How
                    would you like if she was your sister?

                         JOE O'CONNOR
                    Well...she's not my sister. And not
                    take advantage? You're kidding, right?
                    You and that Blue Knight stuff. I think
                    you're spending too much time in that
                    cage grappling with sweaty guys.

                         CHRIS
                    Well...when someone violently resists
                    arrest, what happens? Usually winds up
                    on the ground. I'm preparing not to
                    lose...ever. My instructor's a retired
                    Navy SEAL...talk about a tough dude.

                         JOE O'CONNOR
                    Yeah, well...let's get back to girls.
                    How about this reporter...maybe her?

                         CHRIS
                    We'll see. She's probably just attracted
                    to the uniform.

                         JOE O'CONNOR
                    So what? THAT'S THE IDEA! Come on
                    Chris...get with it. Sometimes you act
                    like a freakin' cloistered monk.

                                        (CONTINUED)

CONTINUED:

Chris chuckles and shrugs.

                    CHRIS
          We'll see.

                    JOE O'CONNOR
          Even this duck thing. I mean, come
          on! Who else would waste his time
          on something that doesn't really matter.

Chris grows pensive as he points to the duck family still
nearby in the shallows.

                    CHRIS
          It really mattered to them.

                    JOE O'CONNOR
          Okay, okay. You did a good thing...
          I'm not saying you didn't. It's just
          ...I don't want to see this job drag
          you down, worrying about everything...
          sweating all the small stuff.

Chris claps his police buddy on the arm.

                    CHRIS
          I appreciate your concern, Joe.
          I really do. Let me call 10-10
          so we can get out of this rain.

The men nod to one another and enter their respective cars.

INT. POLICE DEPARTMENT BRIEFING ROOM

The men are standing for inspection as Sgt. Addison enters
the room and proceeds to the podium, wearing a smirky
expression.

                                        (CONTINUED)

CONTINUED:

                    SGT. ADDISON
          All right, everyone have a seat.
          It's good to know we have heroes
          in this room.

Addison holds up a section of the newspaper featuring
photos of the duck rescue.

                    SGT. ADDISON
                    (sarcastic)
          It's reassuring to know you two
          can be called upon as the Blue Knights
          of the duck world.

Chris and Joe O'Connor display sheepish grins as the rest
of the squad chuckles.

                    SGT. ADDISON
          I'm guessing this was Simone's doing?

                    CHRIS
          That's right, Sarge. I was near the
          lake when I saw what had happened.
          I called in to start an incident card
          and Joe came over to help.

                    SGT. ADDISON
          Did you call the reporter too?

Chris shakes his head.

                    CHRIS
          No. She was driving by and saw
          the patrol cars. I'm guessing
          it was a slow news day for a story.

                                        (CONTINUED)

CONTINUED:

                         SGT. ADDISON
               Did you give her permission to take
               pictures?

                         CHRIS
               I don't have the right to tell her
               not to take pictures.

                         SGT. ADDISON
               Oh really? We'll just have to see
               about that. Wasting department time
               with nonsense. And while we're on
               the subject of nonsense...that tie
               clip you're wearing is departmentally
               unauthorized.

INT. CLOSEUP OF CHRIS' TIE TACK

A resplendently plumed blue knight in full armor with a
closed visor, sword and shield, kneeling in homage.

INT. POLICE DEPARTMENT BRIEFING ROOM

Addison eyes Chris with a stink-eye expression. In an
instant the room's atmosphere grows frigid and no one is
laughing anymore as Addison's ridicule evolves into
scathing contempt.

A rap on the door frame refocuses everyone's attention. A
distinguished, upbeat looking uniformed officer enters the
room. He is CAPTAIN SCOTT.

                         CAPTAIN SCOTT
               Excuse me for interrupting, Sergeant.
               Mind if I have a word with the men?

Addison quickly displays his bootlicking smile.

                         SGT. ADDISON
               Not at all, sir.

                                              (CONTINUED)

CONTINUED:

Captain Scott makes his way to the podium and Sgt. Addison
steps aside.

                    CAPTAIN SCOTT
          I just wanted to take a moment
          to commend Chris and Joe on their
          fine work yesterday.

Captain Scott hesitates as he notices the newspaper on an
adjacent table.

                    CAPTAIN SCOTT
          Looks like you guys already saw
          the article. We've received many
          calls, all of a complimentary nature,
          mostly women, not only from Long Branch
          but all over the state. This morning,
          when the mayor's staff reported to work,
          their office voicemail was filled to
          capacity with positive messages about
          Chris and Joe. We can always use good
          human interest press and on behalf of
          the chief, I want to thank you two for
          your positive work ethic. That's all, men.

Chris and Joe nod as the captain approaches their position
and smiles at them. He stops and gestures towards Chris.

                    CAPTAIN SCOTT
          That's a neat tie clip, Chris. I like it.

                    CHRIS
          Thank you, sir.

Captain Scott leaves the room and all eyes turn back to
Addison, who appears to be making great effort to maintain
his smug bearing.

                    ADDISON
          All right, let's hit the road.

The men file out without a word, leaving Addison standing
there.

INT. PATROL CAR - NIGHT

Chris drives on patrol. His eyes constantly scan for
activity that a police officer should investigate.

                    POLICE CAR RADIO
          Car five-one.

Chris reaches for the microphone.

                    CHRIS
          Car five-one here.

                    POLICE CAR RADIO
          Car five-one...see the woman 1209
          6th Avenue reference missing child.

                    CHRIS
          Five-one ten-four.

Chris drives the patrol car through the darkened streets,
makes a few turns then stops in front of a rundown looking
house. As he scopes the residence he sees a white window
curtain move slightly in an upstairs window, illuminated by
the street light in front of the house. He notices a Harley
Chopper parked beneath a lean-to next to the house.

                    CHRIS
          Five-one is ten-nine.

                    POLICE CAR RADIO
          Ten-four five-one.

Chris exits the patrol car and proceeds to the front door,
knocking four times. Soon a slovenly woman with a snarky
demeanor opens the door. Her name is SUE.

                    SUE
          That was quick.

                    CHRIS
          My name's Officer Simone. Did you
          report a missing child?

                                        (CONTINUED)

CONTINUED:

                    SUE
          You bet I did. You might as well
          come in.

Chris enters the house.

INT. HOUSE - LIVING ROOM

Chris scans the untidy room. A hefty, tattooed, inebriated
looking man wearing a sleeveless tee shirt sits in a lounge
chair holding a bottle of beer, scarcely awake. Two
children watch TV and they both smile when Chris gives a
little wave towards them.

                    SUE
                (loud)
          She's been a problem since she
          found out her father's alive.

                    CHRIS
          She?

                    SUE
          The one I called you about.

                    CHRIS
          All right. What's the child's name
          and how old is she?

                    SUE
          Julie Prescott...9 years old.

                    CHRIS
          And she's your daughter?

                    SUE
          Foster daughter. Why?

                                        (CONTINUED)

CONTINUED:

                         CHRIS
                I need some basic information for
                the report. And your name, please?

                         SUE
                Sue Crespa.

                         CHRIS
                And the foster father's name?

Sue gestures to the hulking man sitting a few feet away.

                         SUE
                Chino Crespa.

Chris eyes Chino, still indifferent and seemingly oblivious
then turns back to Sue. From the angle where he's standing
he doesn't see Chino's eyes flicking towards him every few
seconds.

                         CHRIS
                Mrs. Crespa, when did you last
                see Julie?

                         SUE
                Ummm...about an hour ago.

                         CHRIS
                All right. How many children live here?

                         SUE
                Three.

Chris nods. Something catches his eye and he glances to the
top of the darkened stair case.

INT. HOUSE - TOP OF DARKENED STAIR CASE

Scarcely visible through the darkness is the outline of a
small child at the top of the stairs, watching the activity
in the living room. Chris gives a slight, acknowledging nod
towards the child.

INT. HOUSE - LIVING ROOM

                         CHRIS
          Did you look through the house?

                          SUE
               (overly defensive)
          Of course...do you think I'm an idiot?

                         CHRIS
                  (disarming)
          No ma'am...it's just children are
          creative at times...especially when
          it comes to hiding. You should see
          some of the places I've found kids.
          Mind if I take a look?

Sue folds her arms and looks towards Chino in the lounge
chair.

                          SUE
          The house is a mess.

                         CHRIS
          Oh...that's all right.

Chris reaches for the light switch on the wall at the
bottom of the stairs and flicks on the light.

INT. HOUSE - TOP OF STAIR CASE

The child is no longer at the top of the stairs. Chris
mounts the steps.

INT. HOUSE - HALLWAY AT TOP OF STAIR CASE

Chris stops at each opened bedroom door, flicks on a light
and looks within. At the end of the hallway there's a
closed door which is ajar. He opens the door and sees the
child JULIE PRESCOTT sitting on the steps within leading to
the attic. Holding a small teddy bear dressed in a
Victorian era hat and gown, the child is on the verge of
tears.

                                        (CONTINUED)

CONTINUED:

                    CHRIS
          Hi there. I bet your name is Julie.

The little girl nods.

                    CHRIS
          My name's Officer Simone. There's some
          people downstairs very concerned about
          you.

                    JULIE
          I don't think so.

                    CHRIS
          Why would you think that?

Julie shrugs, fighting back tears.

                    JULIE
          Because they don't care.

She closes he eyes and tears now stream down her cheeks.
Chris eyes her with his empathetic manner and the child
responds.

                    JULIE
          My daddy's in a VA hospital...
          they won't let me see him.

                    CHRIS
          What's his name?

                    JULIE
          Jake Prescott.

Chris holds his hand towards the child.

                                        (CONTINUED)

CONTINUED:

                    CHRIS
          Well...what do you say...you and
          I go downstairs and see what we
          could do about that?

Julie sniffles and takes Chris by the hand. They head
towards the stair case.

                    CHRIS
          Is there anything else you want
          to tell me, Julie?

The child looks at Chris like she wants to say something,
but she just shakes her head.

                    CHRIS
          Are you sure? You can tell me
          anything you want...anything at
          all.

The child hesitates, studying Chris' face and then shakes
her head once more.

INT. HOUSE - LIVING ROOM

Sue hears the footsteps descending the stairs and is
waiting for Chris and Julie.

                    SUE
          (loud, angry and demeaning)
          Always with the tears...what a drama
          queen.

Chris is still holding Julie's hand as they reach the
living room. Sue bends down in a threatening manner towards
Julie, who cringes away behind Chris.

                    SUE
          You've really done it this time!

Julie begins to sob.

                                        (CONTINUED)

CONTINUED:

                         CHRIS
               Please...the child's upset enough.

                          SUE
               And what's that supposed to mean?

                         CHRIS
               That means...please stop shouting.

Chris places himself directly in front of Sue, exuding a
no-nonsense demeanor. Sue notices the change and backs off.
Chris places his hand on Julie's shoulder and guides her so
she's standing alongside him. He keeps his hand on her
shoulder.

                         CHRIS
               It seems Julie has concerns about her
               father.

                          SUE
               She didn't even know about him till a
               few weeks ago.

                         CHRIS
               Is there a reason she shouldn't be
               able to meet with him?

                          SUE
               Sure there is! He's in the East Orange
               VA mental ward. Been there for years.
               Was MIA until the final POW release from
               Nam.

                         CHRIS
               I would think he's allowed visitors.

                          SUE
               I wouldn't know. Besides, he can't speak.
               What kind of visit you think that'd be
               for her?

                                              (CONTINUED)

CONTINUED:

                    JULIE
                    (sad)
          I want to see my daddy.

                    CHRIS
          I'd be willing to make a phone call
          if you'd consider allowing her to
          visit.

                    SUE
          I don't know...I'd have to think about
          that.

Chris removes two business cards from his pocket. He hands
one to Sue.

                    CHRIS
          I'll see what I can find out. In the
          mean time here's my card if you need
          to reach me.

Chris turns to Julie.

                    CHRIS
          I'll be in touch soon, ok Julie?

Smiling, Chris hands a card to the child. The child
hesitantly accepts it, looks it over, then smiles back to
Chris. Chris opens the door to leave.

                    CHRIS
          Good night, everyone.

Chris leaves the house. Sue turns to Julie with cruel
intent and snatches the card from the child's hand.

                    SUE
                    (mean and loud)
          You have your nerve. Who do you think
          you are?

                                        (CONTINUED)

CONTINUED:

Julie begins to cry again. She cringes and backs away as
Sue bends down so her nasty face is close to the child's.

                    SUE
          Don't get your hopes up about
          visiting your loser father. The
          way you've been acting you deserve
          nothing! NOTHING!

There's a knock on the door and Sue turns away from the
child to open it. Standing on the porch a serious looking
Chris regards Sue.

                    CHRIS
          Mrs. Crespa...I could hear you from
          the street. I asked you once to keep
          your voice down.

Chris looks to the sobbing child then back to Sue. He
notices that she's taken his card from the child.

                    SUE
          You've done your good deed. It's
          time you left my house.

                    CHRIS
          I'll leave when I'm satisfied my
          presence is not required for you
          to stop browbeating this child.

His somber manner is not lost on Sue, who backs down from
the police officer for the second time. Chris gestures
towards Julie, who responds by approaching him. Smiling, he
hands her a new card. The child smiles back though
sheepishly.

                    SUE
                (conciliatory)
          Go ahead Julie, watch TV.

(CONTINUED)

CONTINUED:

The child heads into the living room and takes a seat near
the other two children. Chris nods to Sue.

                         CHRIS
                Good night, Mrs. Crespa.

Sue nods and closes the door.

EXT. HOUSE - NIGHT

Chris stands for several moments on the porch. Finally, he
steps down and heads to his patrol car. After taking a
long, final look at the house and the Harley Chopper he
drives off.

INT. POLICE HQ - NIGHT

Chris sits behind a desk, speaking on the phone while
taking notes. There is a flurry of police-related
conversation surging around him.

                         CHRIS
                So...Jake Prescott's never seen
                his daughter Julie?

                    PHONE CONTACT (O.S.)
                Apparently not. It's just a sad case
                all around. He could've gone home for
                good after Khe Sanh. But...he returned
                for his third tour and was captured.
                When Charlie found out who he was it
                was daily torture for five years.
                Something snapped in his head and he
                never spoke again.

                         CHRIS
                I see. He lost his ability to speak
                in Nam?

                                              (CONTINUED)

CONTINUED:

                    PHONE CONTACT (O.S.)
          That's right.

Chris sighs.

                    CHRIS
          How much advance notice would you need
          for a visit?

                    PHONE CONTACT (O.S.)
          The longer the better...at least one
          week. We'd try to prep him first...
          best we could.

                    CHRIS
          Understood. I really appreciate you
          taking the time to speak with me,
          Doctor. I'll be in touch soon.

                    PHONE CONTACT (O.S.)
          Anytime, Officer. Thanks for helping
          one of guys.

                    CHRIS
          You bet.

Chris hangs up the phone and continues writing in his
notebook.

INT. POLICE CRUISER - NIGHT

Chris patrols the streets, his wary eyes always on the
move. Suddenly something catches his attention. He
maneuvers his car curbside and cuts off the headlights.

EXT. DISTRESSED CITY STREET - NIGHT

A young woman, provocatively dressed walks the sidewalk in
front of a liquor store in an area where

                                        (CONTINUED)

CONTINUED:

most of the nearby stores are boarded up. In the recessed
shadows of the building façade men drink out of bottles
hidden within paper bags. Soon a sedan pulls curbside near
the woman. She saunters over to the passenger window and
bends down to engage the driver in conversation. The woman
is Lavanya.

INT. POLICE CRUISER - NIGHT

Chris displays an incredulous expression. He watches for a
few moments then places his car in drive.

EXT. DISTRESSED CITY STREET - NIGHT

Chris pulls the police cruiser behind the sedan while
activating the vehicle's overhead lights. Exiting his car
he walks towards the driver's side. He eyes Lavanya as she
withdraws her head from the passenger window and regards
Chris with a fearful expression. As he closes in on the
male driver he waves Lavayna away from the car.

                    CHRIS
          I need to see your driver's license
          and registration, please.

                    DRIVER
          Why sure, Officer. Is there a problem?

                    CHRIS
          Sure there's a problem. I'll explain
          after you show me your credentials.

The driver fumbles nervously through his wallet. His hands
are shaking when he hands the credentials to Chris. Chris
reviews the credentials.

                    CHRIS
          Sir, you're parked in a no-parking
          zone. What's your business here?

                                        (CONTINUED)

CONTINUED:

                    DRIVER
          Well...I saw my lady friend here
          so I stopped to say hi.

                    CHRIS
          She's your friend, really? What's
          her name?

The driver smiles sheepishly and shrugs. After a long
moment Chris hands him his credentials, eyeing him in a
manner to suggest he knows exactly what is happening.

                    CHRIS
          Go ahead...take off.

                    DRIVER
          Yes sir...thank you, Officer.

The driver slowly drives off. Chris eyes Lavayna on the
sidewalk and approaches her.

                    CHRIS
          What are you doing out here, Lavayna?

Lavayna clasps her hands in front of her, wide-eyed,
scared, avoiding prolonged eye contact with Chris.

                    LAVAYNA
          Well...I was just walking...you know.

                    CHRIS
          Just walking...dressed like that?

Lavayna is unable to maintain eye contact with Chris and
his withering gaze. She looks to the ground.

                    CHRIS
          Who's watching your daughter?

                                        (CONTINUED)

CONTINUED:

Lavayna stifles back tears, involuntarily glancing towards
a small white vehicle parked down the road and across the
street in the parking lot of a closed service station.
Chris follows her eyes.

                    CHRIS
          She's in your car?

Lavayna can't bring herself to look Chris in the face.

                    LAVAYNA
                (whispering)
          Yes.

                    CHRIS
          Give me one reason why I shouldn't
          arrest you and contact Children's
          Services. Just one.

Lavayna begins to cry.

                    LAVAYNA
                (desperate)
          Please Officer Simone...please.
          She's all I have...I have no money
          for food...I'm down to the last two
          jars of baby food...I've been evicted...
          I don't know what else to do...I've
          never done this before.

The normally impassive Chris is livid. He doesn't raise his
voice but his demeanor and tone indicates there's no
question he is beside himself.

                    CHRIS
          So you turn tricks leaving your baby
          daughter parked in your car...in this
          neighborhood? God blessed you with
          a beautiful baby girl...allowed me to
          deliver her to this world for you to do
          this? Shame on you!

                                        (CONTINUED)

CONTINUED:

Lavayna breaks down completely, sobbing into her hands.
Chris eyes her for several long moments and his empathetic
demeanor returns.

                    CHRIS
          Where's your family?

                    LAVAYNA
          Everybody's dead or in jail.

                    CHRIS
          What about your baby's father?

                    LAVAYNA
          Jail.

                    CHRIS
          All right. Here's what we're going
          to do. I'm going to take you to your
          car and you're going to follow me to
          the police station.

                    LAVAYNA
                 (sobbing)
          Are you arresting me?

Chris shakes his head.
                    CHRIS
          No...I'm going to try to get your
          baby and you situated. I need to
          make some phone calls.

Lavayana still sobs. Chris opens the back seat of the
patrol car and ushers her inside. He drives to the closed
gas station where Lavayna has parked her car in the
shadows. They exit the police car and Chris shines his
light in the backseat of Lavayna's car. Her baby daughter
slumbers in the car seat next to a small box containing
baby clothes and two jars of baby food.

                                        (CONTINUED)

CONTINUED:

                    CHRIS
          Follow me to police headquarters.

Lavayna nods and does what she's told.

INT. POLICE HQ LOBBY - NIGHT

Lavayna paces in the lobby holding her slumbering baby.

INT. POLICE HQ - NIGHT

Chris is on the telephone as Sergeant Addison walks by and
eyes him. Just as the sergeant is about to leave the room,
Chris hangs up the phone. The sergeant approaches Chris
with a surly look.

                    SERGEANT ADDISON
               Planning on doing some police work
               tonight?

                    CHRIS
               I'm just finishing up getting a
               young woman and her child situated
               in the Women's Shelter and I'll be
               back on the road.

                    SERGEANT ADDISON
                         (annoyed)
               Women's Shelter? This isn't social
               services.

                    CHRIS
               I know, Sarge. I'm wrapping up and
               heading back on the road.

Chris stands and leaves the room. The sergeant walks to the
window partition where the lobby can be viewed. He watches
as Chris enters the lobby.

INT. POLICE HQ LOBBY

Chris approaches the worried-looking, still provocatively
dressed Lavayna.

                          CHRIS
                Well, I have some good news. There's
                a room for your baby and you at the
                Women's Shelter in Tinton Falls. I
                wrote down the directions for you.

                          LAVAYNA
                (tearful)
                I know where it is...that's a nice
                place. I don't know how to thank you.

                          CHRIS
                Just get yourself together and do
                what's right for your child. Here's
                a few dollars to hold you over until
                you get settled.

Chris places some folded money into Lavayna's hand.

                          LAVAYNA
                Thank you, Officer Simone!

Lavayna embraces Chris with her free arm. Just then her
baby awakens and looks up wide-eyed at Chris. Chris smiles
and touches the baby's hand.

                          CHRIS
                Hello there!

The baby smiles back at Chris. In the background, Sergeant
Addison views the scene through the lobby window, a dark
scowl on his face.

INT. POLICE HQ SHIFT COMMANDER OFFICE

Sergeant Addison is standing at the office doorway with
folded arms. When Chris emerges from the lobby he calls
out.

                                            (CONTINUED)

CONTINUED:

                    SGT. ADDISON
         Simone...in my office.

Chris enters the office and Sgt. Addison closes the door.

                    SGT. ADDISON
         Have a seat.

Chris sits down and Sgt. Addison takes the seat behind the desk.

                    SGT. ADDISON
         Do you want to tell me what's going
         on with you and that chippy visiting
         here?

                    CHRIS
         Chippy?

                    SGT. ADDISON
         That girl with the baby. The one you
         handed a wad of cash.

                    CHRIS
         She's been evicted. She was broke so
         I gave her a few bucks.

                    SGT. ADDISON
         Just like that...out of the goodness of
         your heart?

                    CHRIS
         Well...yes.

                    SGT. ADDISON
         I'm not buying it...not buying it at all.

(CONTINUED)

CONTINUED:

                    CHRIS
          It's the truth. Her baby was the one
          I helped deliver during the blizzard
          with Joe O'Connor.

                    SGT. ADDISON
          Still not buying it.

                    CHRIS
          I'm not sure what you're implying,
          Sergeant.

                    SGT. ADDISON
          Nobody hands money over to someone
          dressed like that for no reason.

                    CHRIS
          She needed help tonight and I helped
          her. Simple as that. Haven't you ever
          helped someone who needed it, especially
          someone with a child with no place else
          to turn?

                    SGT. ADDISON
                    (smugly)
          This isn't about me, Simone.

Chris does not respond as the two men glare at one another.
Finally Sgt. Addison breaks the silence.

                    SGT. ADDISON
          Go back on the road, Simone.

Chris leaves the office without uttering another word.

INT. HOUSE - BEDROOM

Little Julie Prescott prepares herself for bed, slipping a
nightgown over her head. She turns around and is startled
by the hulking figure regarding her from the doorway, the
same individual resting in the lounge chair earlier when
Chris was present, CHINO CRESPA.

                                              (CONTINUED)

CONTINUED:

                    CHINO
          I'll be in a little later to tuck
          you in.

A sickening smile adorns Chino's face as he turns away and
disappears into the hallway. Julie's facial expression and
body language reveals she's terrified of Chino. She reaches
under her bed and pulls out a small, pink vinyl little girl
suitcase, places some clothing within along with a small
glass jar containing coins. She re-dresses herself and puts
on her coat, shuts the bedroom light, grabs her teddy bear
from the bed and climbs out of the window.

EXT. SIDEWALK - NIGHT

Julie walks down the sidewalk along the darkened streets,
hugging her teddy bear. It's obvious she's scared. She
cautiously crosses at the corner of each deserted street.
In the distance the vague outline of a train station is
visible as a public bus turns into the adjacent parking
area. Julie heads in that direction. She stops at an
outdoor telephone, removes Chris' card from her coat pocket
and is about to use the phone when she notices an overhead
wire has been cut.

                    JULIE
                (barely a whisper)
          Oh no.

She places the card back into her pocket and continues
toward the train station where two more buses have entered.

Suddenly, the distant sound of a loud motorcycle exhaust
can be heard. Wide-eyed with fear, Julie looks back in the
direction from where she had come.

EXT. STREET - NIGHT

A solitary headlight is moving in Julie's direction. The
motorcycle's exhaust grows louder still.

EXT. STREET - NIGHT

Julie quickly crosses the street with her little suitcase
and teddy bear and runs into the train station near the
path of the moving buses. Suddenly a bus horn sounds,
blaring loud, followed by the screech of brakes.

INT. PATROL CAR - NIGHT

Chris is parked with the headlights off, watching a small
group of men gathered in the distressed area where he had
encountered Lavayna earlier. The men appear to be just
talking. Chris is about to leave when the police radio
interrupts the quiet.

                    POLICE CAR RADIO
               All cars...10-15 with injury...child
               struck by a bus...Long Branch Train
               Station.

                    CHRIS
               Car Five-one 10-4.

Chris activates the police car's overhead lights and speeds
away. The group he's watching disperses, startled by the
sudden police presence.

EXT. TRAIN STATION PARKING LOT - NIGHT

A crowd has gathered near the train platform steps. Another
police car is already there. Chris maneuvers his car nearby
and hops out. As he approaches the crowd he notices the
teddy bear with the Victorian hat and gown resting on the
ground illuminated in the headlights of his patrol car.
Visibly shaken, Chris bends down to pick up the bear. At
that moment, a loud motorcycle exhaust can be heard
sounding from the main street. At first, Chris doesn't seem
to notice, but suddenly he moves towards the roadway.
There's a long line of visual obstructions caused by the
buses. By the time he reaches the roadway, all he could see
is a solitary red taillight disappearing into the night.
Slowly, he turns back towards the crowd.

                                        FADE TO BLACK

FADE IN FROM BLACK

INT. CHURCH RECTORY

An obviously doleful Chris sits opposite Father Armand.

                    CHRIS
          I should have taken her out of the house.
          The signs were all there. If I had taken
          her out she'd still be alive...and maybe
          she would have opened up...about that
          other stuff.

                    FATHER ARMAND
          You can't always second guess yourself
          Chris. How many houses have you visited
          where your instincts trigger but legally
          you can't take action? I'm sure that
          happens quite often.

                    CHRIS
          Yeah...but not where a little girl
          winds up dead.

Chris tears up and he places his hand over his eyes.

                    CHRIS
          Father...I just know that slob Chino
          Crespa was the one...the one who molested
          her. That poor kid was trying to get
          away from him...probably trying to head
          to the V.A. hospital to see her father.

                    FATHER ARMAND
          I trust your intuition. But you,
          especially as an officer of the law,
          can't cross the line without absolute
          proof. The detectives questioned
          this...Crespa and his wife and came up
          with nothing. The post mortem provided
          nothing to link him conclusively.

                                        (CONTINUED)

CONTINUED:

                    CHRIS
          I know, Father...I know. But still,
          I have no doubt on his one.

                                        FADE TO BLACK

FADE IN FROM BLACK

EXT. HOSPITAL BUILDING - DAY

A large blue sign with white lettering stands prominently
alongside the driveway leading onto hospital grounds
stating: **U.S. Department of Veterans Affairs**
                      East Orange, NJ

Chris is seen driving a dark sedan into the parking lot.

INT. INTERVIEW ROOM

Chris is sitting at a table, a small cloth bag resting
before him. He is not in uniform. After a few moments, the
door opens and a small, unkempt, disheveled looking man
with a confused look is led in by a hospital attendant. The
man's name is JAKE PRESCOTT. Chris stands up and offers his
hand and the man offers a return shake.

                    CHRIS
          Mr. Prescott. My name is Chris Simone.
          I'm a police officer with the Long Branch
          Police Department.

Jake regards Chris with no change in expression.

                    CHRIS
          I understand that Dr. Snyder has
          already spoken to you... about Julie.

                                        (CONTINUED)

CONTINUED:

Jake tilts his head a bit.

                    CHRIS
          I want to tell you how sorry I am
          for your loss. I only met her once
          but I could tell you that your daughter
          was a sweet, beautiful child. I brought
          a few things of hers I know she'd want
          you to have.

Chris reaches into the bag and removes Julie's teddy bear
with the Victorian gown and hat and then a small photo of a
smiling Julie from a happier time within a frame stating
the words 'I LOVE MY DADDY'. He places the items before
Jake. Jake's eyes open wide as he studies the items.

                    CHRIS
          They're yours, Mr. Prescott.

Jake reaches with a trembling hand and gathers the bear and
photo so the items are resting on the table directly before
him. His eyes move slowly back and forth between
the two. He finally touches the bear's gown with his
fingertips and then picks up the photo and studies it.

Chris notices that Jake's eyes are full of tears. The two
men share the silence.

                                        FADE TO BLACK

FADE IN FROM BLACK

EXT. REAR OF STRIP MALL BUILDING - NIGHT

Jake Prescott stands in the shadows eyeing the backdoor of
a business illuminated by a solitary light bulb. Jake is
wearing a drab field jacket adorned with Gunnery Sergeant
stripes displaying the telltale crossed M-1 Garand rifles.

                                        (CONTINUED)

CONTINUED:

A Silver Star military medallion is pinned to the chest of
his jacket. Shivering, he turns up his collar and cups his
gnarled hands to his mouth and blows into them.

EXT. BACKDOOR OF BUSINESS - NIGHT

The door opens and out steps a husky, dark haired man
dressed in white with flour-dusted hands carrying two paper
bags which he quickly deposits upon a metal can a few feet
from the door. Marine Corps insignia and 'Semper Fidelis'
tattoos adorn both of his forearms. Pizzeria equipment is
visible inside the door. Despite the cold the man does not
hurry inside, instead lingering, gazing into the
surrounding shadows; a long, knowing look. Finally, the man
turns and heads back inside, closing the door.

Jake emerges from the shadows, grabs the two bags and
disappears. He doesn't notice the husky, dark haired man
watching him through a small window next to the rear door.

EXT. REAR OF STRIP MALL BUILDING - NIGHT

Jake disappears into a small crawl space entrance.

INT. CRAWLSPACE - DARK

Jake lights a candle, opens the bags of food and begins
eating in a ravenous manner. He consumes pizza, soup and
cheese while drinking from a green bottle of sparkling
water to wash it down. Julie's photo and teddy bear are
propped up before him. Every few moments Jake glances at
both.

                                            DISSOLVE TO:

INT. CRAWLSPACE ILLUMINATED BY CANDLELIGHT

Jake dozes in a sitting position.

INT. POLICE DEPARTMENT BRIEFING ROOM

Standing behind a podium Sgt. Addison gives the daily
briefing to the police squad starting the new shift.

                    SGT. ADDISON
          I'm not sure why this was sent to us
          but there's an APB from the East Orange
          VA about an escaped mental patient...a war
          veteran named Jake Prescott. Disappeared
          from the hospital 3 days ago.

Chris was staring down at his notepad but abruptly looks up
when Jake Prescott's name is mentioned. Chris raises his
hand to get the sergeant's attention.

                    SGT. ADDISON
          Yes, Simone.

                    CHRIS
          He's the father of the little girl killed
          at the train station.

                    SGT. ADDISON
          I see...he's described as a white male,
          Five feet eight, slim build...brown hair,
          disheveled appearance...mute...Silver Star
          recipient...last seen wearing a military
          field jacket with Marine Gunnery Sergeant
          stripes. Well...I'm not sure why he'd be here
          in Long Branch but he's a war hero so if we
          find him let's treat him right. A sleet
          storm is supposed to hit so hopefully the
          streets will be empty. All right fellas...
          that's it...let's be safe out there.

The police officers stand and break into small talk as they
exit the room.

INT. CRAWLSPACE ILLUMINATED BY CANDLELIGHT

Jake is still dozing when the sound of an approaching car
reaches him. Quickly he blows out the candle.

EXT. DRIVEWAY REAR OF STRIP MALL BUILDING - NIGHT

A dark sedan with headlights shut off stops beside a
dumpster located a few feet away from the crawlspace
entrance. A young woman exits the vehicle, opens the
dumpster door and without fanfare pitches a bundle within.
She hastily re-enters the vehicle and the car quickly
leaves the scene.

EXT. REAR OF STRIP MALL BUILDING - NIGHT

Jake slowly emerges from the crawlspace and proceeds to the
dumpster. Opening the door, he reaches inside and suddenly
recoils grasping a plastic bag containing an object.

EXT. CLOSEUP OF PLASTIC BAG IN JAKE'S HAND

A newborn baby's form is clearly visible through the
transparent plastic.

EXT. NEXT TO DUMPSTER - NIGHT

Gasping, Jake lurches backwards, nearly dropping the
infant. He composes himself and proceeds back to the
crawlspace.

INT. CRAWLSPACE - DARK

Jake relights the candle and quickly removes the baby from
the bag and wraps the child inside an old, discarded towel.
Picking up Julie's photo and bear he places them in his
pocket then blows out the candle.

EXT. CRAWLSPACE ENTRANCE - NIGHT

Jake stands, places the baby inside his jacket and zippers
it shut. He walks over to the back door of the pizzeria and
knocks on the door but there's no answer and as he peeks
through a small adjacent window the interior is dark.

EXT. DRIVEWAY REAR OF STRIP MALL BUILDING - NIGHT

Jake walks until he emerges from the rear of the strip
mall.

EXT. STRIP MALL FACADE - NIGHT

As Jake rounds the corner the Long Branch Train Station
where Julie died comes into view across the street from the
strip mall. The train platform is deserted and there are no
idling buses or taxi cabs.

EXT. SIDEWALK - NIGHT

Jake walks until he comes upon a pay phone, the same phone
his daughter Julie tried to use the night she died. He hits
0 for operator and then notices that the overhead wire is
severed. As an icy sleet begins to fall he grimaces and
trudges on.

EXT. NIGHT

Jake continues walking through the darkened streets. The
sleet has developed into a furious downward assault that
tingles like shards of broken glass upon the frozen,
deserted pavement. The wind approaches gale fury as Jake
plods on.

EXT. DARKENED CHURCH - NIGHT

Jake mounts the icy steps and tugs on the door handles to
no avail. Jake climbs down the steps and staggers around
the side of the church towards the darkened rectory in the
rear.

EXT. DARKENED RECTORY

Jake knocks softly on the front door. When there's no
answer he raps harder and harder until he's pounding with a
closed fist. A light appears upstairs. Moments later the
porch lamp lights up and a small, bespectacled man eyes
Jake intently through the opened door. The man is the
church PASTOR.

(CONTINUED)

CONTINUED:

                    PASTOR
          It's a little late...don't you think?

Suddenly the bell in the church steeple tolls twice.

                    JAKE
          Buh...Buh.

Jake opens his field jacket and hands the slumbering baby
over to the bewildered pastor.

                    PASTOR
          A baby! Sweet Jesus! Where did you
          find a baby on a night like this?

Jake gestures with his hand towards the street.

                    JAKE
          Buh...Buh...Duh...Duh.

                    PASTOR
          Why don't you come in out of the
          cold...the police will want you
          to show them where you found this
          baby.

                    JAKE
          Nah...Nah...Puh...Puh.

Jake shakes his head and retreats from the door, limping
off into the frozen night.

                    PASTOR
          The police won't harm you!

EXT. DESERTED ROAD - NIGHT

Jake sees the slow-moving headlights and accompanying alley
and spot beams of a police cruiser moving towards him.
Quickly, he scurries down a nearby culvert.

EXT. DRAINAGE PIPE WITHIN CULVERT - NIGHT

Jake crawls into a large drainage pipe.

INT. DRAINAGE PIPE - DARK

A few moments later the sound of a car engine and the
diffused light from the police cruiser passes. Darkness and
silence reign again, except for the tingle of sleet
striking the culvert and the exterior of the drainage pipe.

Jake relights his candle. Removing Julie's photo and teddy
bear from his pockets he rests them near the candle. For
several moments, he shivers violently then closes his eyes
as weariness and exhaustion set upon him.

EXT. DARKENED ABYSS - JAKE'S EUPHORIC VISION

Dazzling, golden light closes upon Jake. At the core of the
radiance is a small child, a beautiful girl with long, dark
hair and outstretched arms, glowingly beckoning him forth.
As she approaches it is obviously Julie's spirit.

                    JULIE'S SPIRIT
          Daddy...where have you been?

Jake reaches forth, embracing her, looking into her eyes,
by the beaming expression on his face not ever knowing such
happiness.

Together, arm in arm they ascend into the heavenly
brightness high up above in tandem with an angelic
resonance.

                                        FADE TO BLACK

FADE IN FROM BLACK

EXT. STREET ABOVE THE CULVERT - MORNING - DAY

Two black and white police cruisers are parked above the
culvert. A third police car arrives at the scene. Chris
steps out and walks to the culvert guardrail and looks over
the side.

EXT. CULVERT BOTTOM - MORNING

Two uniformed police officers, one young and the other a
seasoned street cop holding flashlights in gloved hands
wave up to Chris.

EXT. STREET ABOVE THE CULVERT - MORNING - DAY

Chris nods back and proceeds to climb carefully down the
sleet-coated drop.

EXT. CULVERT BOTTOM - MORNING

                    OLDER COP
          Thought you got off at seven?

                    CHRIS
          I did, but they caught me before I left
          and sent me here to make a possible I.D.
          What've we got?

                    YOUNG COP
            (pointing to the drainpipe)
          Just some bum crawling inside a rat hole
          to die. Fits the description of a subject
          who handed over a newborn infant girl to
          Pastor Ryan at zero two hundred... he must
          have wandered here from the church. A guy
          walking his dog found him and called us...

                    OLDER COP
          Yeah...not exactly a Currier and Ives moment.

Chris moves to the drainpipe opening and shines his
flashlight within.

INT. DRAINPIPE - DARK

The flashlight beam illuminates Jake's frozen body. His
eyes are locked heavenward yet unclouded by death's
absolute embrace, seemingly in a final, peaceful bliss.
Frozen sleet covers the unkempt hair and beard. The Silver
Star medallion is still pinned to the chest of his field
jacket. The teddy bear, Julie's photo and burned down
candle round out the disheartening vision.

EXT. DRAINPIPE - MORNING

Chris turns away ashen-faced.

                    CHRIS
          Jesus Christ!

The cops are startled by Chris Simone's reaction.

                    OLDER COP
          Who is that in there?

                    CHRIS
          That man...he's no bum...U.S. Marine
          with three tours of duty in 'Nam. Won
          the Silver Star. When he was captured
          during his third tour Charlie found out
          he was a war hero and tortured him daily
          ...beat him so badly he lost his ability
          to speak. Finally, back in the states after
          a long, drawn out convalescence only to
          find out his wife was killed in an accident
          and his daughter placed in foster care. He
          tried for custody but a mute, disabled,
          broke, former POW with post-traumatic stress
          disorder didn't stand much chance in court.
          And last week...

Chris chokes up momentarily and catches himself.

                    CHRIS
          Last week his little daughter was killed
          at the train station. She ran away from
          her foster home...God knows why. She was
          probably heading to see him at the V.A.

Chris looks at the faces of the two cops and sees they are
saddened.

                    CHRIS
          The detective should be here soon for
          photos. I'll let him know who this man
          is. That should expedite things a bit.
          He'll soon be on his way to Arlington
          National Cemetery. Thank-you fellas.

                                        (CONTINUED)

CONTINUED:

Chris climbs out of the culvert.

The two cops stand in silence, eyes flicking every few
moments towards the drainpipe. The older of the two finally
speaks.

                         OLDER COP
               Guess I shouldn't complain about shift
               work.

                         YOUNG COP
               Yeah...guess I shouldn't complain about
               anything...at all.

The men remain silent as the wind moans overhead and the
sun edges higher. Golden rays dazzle the view through ice-
coated tree branches swaying high above the culvert.

EXT. CITY STREET - DUSK

Chino Crespa rides his Harley Chopper through a deserted
city street at a high rate of speed. He glances in his
rearview mirror and does a retake.

EXT. CLOSEUP OF HARLEY'S REARVIEW MIRROR

A police cruiser is right on his tail with activated
overhead lights.

EXT. CITY STREET - DUSK

Chino Crespa maneuvers his Harley curbside as the police
cruiser does the same.

                                              (CONTINUED)

CONTINUED:

After a few moments, Chris exits the cruiser and approaches
Crespa, who has remained straddled on his Harley after
removing his helmet which strongly resembles an SS Storm
Trooper's headgear. The extreme size disparity between the
two men is plain to see.

                         CHRIS
               Driver's license, registration and
               insurance card.

                         CHINO
                    (cocky and defiant)
               I know I wasn't speeding.

Chris remains silent as Chino removes the requested
documents from his oversized wallet attached by a chain to
his belt. He hands the paperwork to Chris.

                         CHRIS
               The reason you were stopped is that
               you failed to utilize your directional
               signal when turning from Joline to Central.
               You also didn't come to a complete stop
               two blocks ago at the stop sign. You'll be
               issued a summons for each violation.

                         CHINO
               That's a crock, man!

                         CHRIS
               You may contest the charges by contact-
               ing the municipal court and entering a
               not guilty plea. Wait here.

Chris walks back and enters his patrol car.

INT. POLICE CRUISER

Chris picks up the radio mic.

                         CHRIS
               Car five-one to headquarters. Ten-Eleven
               for a driver's license and NCIC check.

                         POLICE RADIO
               Go ahead, five-one.

                         CHRIS
               Subject's name is Chino Crespa. NJ
               drivers license C as in Charley,
               1-6-4-9...6-3-7-4-5...0-3-6-2-2.

                         POLICE RADIO
               Copy that five-one...standby.

Chris fills out the motor vehicle summonses.

EXT. ROADWAY - DUSK

Chino remains seated on his Harley with folded arms,
brooding

INT. POLICE CRUISER

                         POLICE RADIO
               Car five-one...no wants or warrants...
               no record of arrest...driver's license
               valid...no points.

                         CHRIS
                         (frowning)
               Five-one roger that.

Chris exits the patrol car.

EXT. ROADWAY - DUSK

Chris approaches Chino.

(CONTINUED)

CONTINUED:

                    CHRIS
          You've been issued a summons for
          failing to utilize your directional
          signal and failing to come to a
          complete stop at a stop sign. If you
          wish to contest the charges your court
          date is indicated on the back of the
          summons.

Chino snatches the summons and documents from Chris.

                    CHINO
          You pigs are all the same.

Chris makes direct eye contact with Chino.

                    CHRIS
          Rest assured...your day's coming
          soon...and I don't mean in a good
          way.

                    CHINO
          You threatenin' me?

                    CHRIS
              (through clenched teeth)
          Take it anyway you want...I know what
          you did to that little girl...if you
          don't know what karma is...you're going
          to find out.

Chino is visibly rattled by the reference to little Julie
Prescott.

                    CHINO
          You can't prove nothin'.

                    CHRIS
          That's the beauty of karma...
          nothing needs to be 'proven'
          because it's already a done deal.

                                        (CONTINUED)

CONTINUED:

Chris backs away without taking his eyes off Chino. He
enters the patrol car. Chino starts up his Harley. He uses
his directional signal as he motors the bike slowly ahead.

                                        FADE TO BLACK

FADE IN FROM BLACK

INT. POLICE CRUISER - DAY

Chris is on routine patrol.

                    POLICE RADIO
               Unit five-one and any units nearby.
               10-15 - a car was just driven into
               Takanassee Lake - report of trapped
               passengers.

                    CHRIS
               Five-one ten - four...en route.

Chris activates his overhead lights and yelping siren.

EXT. SEMI-FROZEN POND - DAYLIGHT

The same small lake where Chris learned to ice skate with
his father is the scene of a motor vehicle accident, where
ice floes permeate the semi-frozen surface. A crowd has
gathered on the shore. With the nearby fire department
rescue fire horn sounding ominously loud and without
relent, Chris is the first officer on the scene. He sees
the car is beginning to sink about thirty feet from shore.
A couple of young men abandon their rescue efforts and
begin swimming back to shore. Chris strips down to his
shorts and swims out to the car, pounds the already cracked
rear window with a rock resting on the trunk, ostensibly
left by the early rescue attempt, breaks the glass and
reaches in and pulls out an elderly man to safety. As Chris
brings the man ashore, the man cries out.

                                        (CONTINUED)

CONTINUED:

                    ELDERLY MAN
              My sister's still in the car!

Chris turns just as the car slides beneath the surface.
Without hesitation, he jumps back in, swims to where the
car had disappeared and submerges. By this time there are
many onlookers. Additional police cars appear at the scene.
After several anxious moments, Chris surfaces and begins
stroking to shore with the unconscious, elderly woman
driver in tow. The onlookers break into applause. Several
police officers have entered the water and assist Chris by
taking the woman off his hands. First-Aiders begin CPR on
the woman as a shivering Chris watches from the shore of
the pond. After several frantic moments, the woman opens
her eyes, coughs out a large quantity of water and begins
crying hysterically. Finally, Chris is handed a blanket by
fellow Officer Joe O'Connor.

                    JOE O'CONNOR
              That really took a set of stones,
              Chris!

                    CHRIS
                (teeth chattering)
              Man...I am freezing! Let me find my
              clothes and get out of here. Would
              you handle the report for me, Joe?

                    JOE O'CONNOR
              Sure Chris...you got it.

Gathering his uniform clothing Chris heads back to the
police cruiser as the first aid squad places the very much
alive elderly couple involved in the accident into the back
of an ambulance.

INT. POLICE DEPARTMENT LOCKER ROOM

Chris is nearly dressed as he stands before his locker, a
towel around his shoulders. There's background chatter on

                                              (CONTINUED)

CONTINUED:

his portable police radio about a domestic dispute. His
hair is still damp as he flexes his hands open and closed
then claps them together before securing his gun belt in
place.

                    POLICE PORTABLE RADIO
                        (highly excited)
            10-48! 10-48! Officers need assistance
            1209 6th Avenue!

Chris slams his locker shut and hurries out of the room.

EXT. CITY STREET - DAY

Chris drives the police cruiser rapidly with lights and
siren.

EXT. HOUISE - DAY

Chris sees another patrol car along with an unmarked
detective vehicle haphazardly parked as he maneuvers his
patrol car in front of 1209 6th Avenue. As he jumps out of
the car shouts and bellowing are heard emanating from
within the house. He notices the Harley Chopper parked
beneath the lean-to next to the house.

                          CHRIS
              Five-one is 10-9. Send more help!

INT. HOUSE - LIVING ROOM

Chris enters a scene of complete chaos with overturned
furniture everywhere. Julie Prescott's foster mother Sue
has been beaten to a bloody pulp as her hysterical children
huddle over her. A bloodied Joe O'Connor is collapsed on
the floor unconscious as Chino Crespa is in the process of
throttling a plain-clothes detective. He has the man in a
tight headlock and is smashing his huge fist in devastating
uppercuts into the man's face. Chris winds up with his

                                              (CONTINUED)

CONTINUED:

nightstick two-handed and cracks Chino on the kneecap,
causing the man to bellow as his leg buckles. Chino drops
the detective and rushes Chris flailing his arms. Chris
swings his nightstick and smashes Chino's hands but the
huge man bulls through and pins him against the wall,
throwing haymakers. Chino clamps his hands around Chris'
throat and Chris responds by thrusting his nightstick into
Chino's throat and his knee sharply into his groin, causing
Chino to loosen his grip. Chris throws several overhand
hammer fists, shattering Chino's nose, followed by elbows
to his jaw.

With police sirens yelping in the distance Chris hits Chino
in the throat a second time and wriggles loose though his
nightstick drops. Chino tries to clamp down but Chris hits
a beautifully timed wrestling duck under and maneuvers
himself onto Chino's back. He sinks his right arm so the
crook of his elbow squeezes around the huge man's throat
and with his right hand clasps the inside of his upper left
arm so that he now has a rear naked choke hold. Chino tries
to thrash loose and smashes Chris into the wall repeatedly,
breaking sheetrock but Chris clamps down with all his
strength and suddenly Chino's legs aren't working and he
drops to his knees. Chino's eyes bulge and he makes
gurgling sounds as he collapses.

                    CHRIS
              (through clenched teeth)
          This one's for Julie.

Chris grimaces as he squeezes with all his might. There's
an audible cracking noise and he's still clamping down as
two uniformed officers burst into the room. Chris places
his knee into Chino's back as he releases his choke hold.

                    CHRIS
              (breathing hard)
          Hook him up!

                                        (CONTINUED)

CONTINUED:

The two uniformed officers quickly do as they're told and Chris rolls to his back, gasping for air as he holds his hands to his head. His face is bloodied.

The room quickly fills with police officers who proceed to attend the injured. A female police officer removes the two terrified children from the scene. As Chris sits up he feels a hand on his shoulder. He looks up into the concerned face of Captain Scott.

                    CAPTAIN SCOTT
          You've had quite a tour of duty today,
          Chris. You're taking the rest of the
          shift off...get yourself checked out.

                    CHRIS
                    (wincing)
          I'm alright sir...little banged up
          maybe. Might have a couple cracked
          ribs...and a busted nose.

                    CAPTAIN SCOTT
          Don't worry, we'll find out for sure.

                    CHRIS
          Yes sir. How's the woman and the other
          guys doing?

                    CAPTAIN SCOTT
          I don't know yet...they're lucky you
          showed up when you did. How did you
          take that monster by yourself?

Captain Scott gestures towards the prostrate Chino Crespa who's gurgling and moaning while slowly shaking his head side to side.

                              (CONTINUED)

CONTINUED:

Chris shrugs.

                    CHRIS
          Everything happened so fast...
          I'm guessing the good Lord knew
          which of us was on His side.

Captain Scott smiles and pats Chris on the shoulder, then
offers his hand and helps Chris rise slowly to his feet.

                    CAPTAIN SCOTT
          Indeed...I'll tell you what...I'll
          drive you to the hospital myself.

                    CHRIS
          Yes sir...I'd appreciate that.

The two men leave the bustling room now filled with cops,
first-aiders and stretchers to the sound of emergency radio
chatter blaring without relent.

                                        FADE TO BLACK

FADE IN FROM BLACK

INT. HOSPITAL EMERGENCY ROOM

A battered Chris is resting on the hospital bed. He looks
around and slowly sits up, grimacing. He places his feet
down and stands. Moving towards the center of the room, he
looks at each bed until he finds Joe O'Connor resting next
to a monitor with his eyes swollen shut and a busted-up
appearance. Chris moves close, sadness upon his face.

                    CHRIS
                 (whispering)
          Joe...can you hear me?

                                        (CONTINUED)

CONTINUED:

Joe stirs a little and faces towards the sound of Chris'
voice though his eyes remain closed.

                    JOE
            (barely a whisper)
        Chris? Is that you?

Chris rests his hand on Joe's arm.

                    CHRIS
        Hey buddy. How you feeling?

                    JOE
        Terrible but the nurse gave me
        a shot...it's starting to work.
        That guy hurt me bad...I thought
        he was going to kill me.

                    CHRIS
        Yeah...I felt the same. But I
        don't think he'll hurt anyone
        again anytime soon.

                    JOE
        Did you shoot him?

                    CHRIS
        No...thought about it but too
        many kids...people in the room.

                    JOE
        So what did you do?

                    CHRIS
        Well...let's just say those moves
        I practice in the cage grappling
        with sweaty guys finally came in
        mighty handy.

Joe starts to chuckle and Chris follows suit. At that
moment, a NURSE walks in.

                                        (CONTINUED)

CONTINUED:

                    NURSE
          Good to see you guys laughing
          a bit.

                    CHRIS
          I'm going to hang out if it's ok.

                    NURSE
          Sure. I'll be out of here in a minute.

The nurse checks Joe's face up close and then the monitor
before making an entry on Joe's clipboard. She smiles and
continues her rounds.

                    CHRIS
          Greg's probably in here somewhere.
          I should go find him.

                    JOE
          Chris...would you stay here for a
          while...please?

                    CHRIS
          Sure...I'll go check on Greg in a
          little bit.

Chris pulls a chair close to Joe's bed and sits down.

                              FADE TO BLACK

FADE IN FROM BLACK

INT. CAPTAIN SCOTT'S OFFICE

Captain Scott sits at his desk reviewing documents. Sgt.
Addison approaches and knocks on the door frame.

                    SGT. ADDISON
          You wanted to see me, Captain?

                              (CONTINUED)

CONTINUED:

                    CAPTAIN SCOTT
          Yes...come in and close the door.

Sgt. Addison enters the room and Capt. Scott gestures for
him to sit down. Sgt. Addison smirks as he notices a
picture of Jesus sitting with two small children upon His
lap amongst the bevy of police citations covering the wall
behind the captain.

                    CAPTAIN SCOTT
          I've been reviewing your I.A.
          complaint against Chris Simone.
          I must say it is definitely a
          C-L-M.

                    SGT. ADDISON
          C-L-M sir?

                    CAPTAIN SCOTT
          Career Limiting Move.

Sgt. Addison shifts in his seat, his expression indicating
a smug satisfaction.

                    SGT. ADDISON
          I thought so too, sir. That's why
          I wrote him up when I saw him handing
          money to that hooker in the lobby.

                    CAPTAIN SCOTT
          The career limiting move I'm referring
          to is yours.

                    SGT. ADDISON
                    (surprised)
          Mine?

                    CAPTAIN SCOTT
          I did my own investigation concerning
          the charges you submitted and found out
          Chris was helping a desperate young

                                              (CONTINUED)

CONTINUED:

>   girl half out of her mind...evicted
>   ...broke...with a hungry baby to feed
>   and nowhere to turn. It was Chris who
>   offered a helping hand in her time of
>   need. And what does he get for his
>   compassion? YOU...writing him up on an
>   Internal Affairs complaint. That's
>   certainly some reward for being kind-
>   hearted.

Now Sgt. Addison squirms uncomfortably.

>   SGT. ADDISON
>   I thought I was doing the right thing.

>   CAPTAIN SCOTT
>   It certainly was not the 'right thing'
>   and reflects poorly on your leadership
>   qualities...and the lack thereof.
>
>   You're always supposed to look out for
>   your men, Sergeant. They risk their lives
>   every time they wear that uniform and
>   shouldn't be looking over their shoulders
>   for this type of garbage. And I know for
>   a fact this isn't the first time you've
>   gone out of your way to stick it to him
>   over utter nonsense...like your derogatory
>   ethnic comments and reprimands for
>   unauthorized tie clips.

>   SGT. ADDISON
>   (indignant)
>   I suppose he's complained to you?

>   CAPTAIN SCOTT
>   Never...not a peep. But don't think
>   for a moment that I don't have my
>   finger on the pulse of everything
>   happening around here.

(CONTINUED)

CONTINUED:

Captain Scott seems to be on the verge of losing his cool.
He takes a deep breath.

                    CAPTAIN SCOTT
          I don't want to raise my voice.
          We're done here...for now. You're
          dismissed.

Captain Scott gestures toward the door and a dejected Sgt.
Addison stands and leaves the room.

INT. HALLWAY - OUTSIDE OF CAPTAIN SCOTT'S OFFICE

As Sgt. Addison exits the captain's office he sees Chris
Simone in plain clothes sitting on an adjacent bench. Chris
nods but after the initial look Sgt. Addison avoids eye
contact and disappears through a door at the end of the
hall. As Chris looks around he sees Captain Scott standing
at his office door.

                    CAPTAIN SCOTT
                      (upbeat)
          Come on in, Chris.

INT. CAPTAIN SCOTT'S OFFICE

                    CAPTAIN SCOTT
          Please have a seat.

                    CHRIS
          Thank you, sir.

Slowly Chris sits down as Captain Scott closes the door. He
sees the Jesus picture and smiles. His face is still
bruised from his fight with Chino Crespa. The bridge of his
nose now resembles that of a pugilist a la Rocky Marciano.

                                        (CONTINUED)

CONTINUED:

                    CAPTAIN SCOTT
          How are those ribs?

                    CHRIS
          A little sore, sir, but coming along.

                    CAPTAIN SCOTT
          That's good to hear. The Department of
          Justice contacted us regarding 'Chino
          Crespa' and I wanted to provide you with
          an update of what I've learned so far.
          Please keep in mind this is confidential.

                    CHRIS
          Of course, Captain.

Captain Scott leans forward a bit.

                    CAPTAIN SCOTT
          Chino Crespa' is the alias provided
          by the DOJ for an individual assigned
          to their witness protection program.
          His real name is Moriah Barge.

                    CHRIS
               (nodding, intense)
          I knew something was wrong when
          I ran him through N.C.I.C. and DMV
          and nothing came up. There's no way
          someone like him would have no
          record...no way.

                    CAPTAIN SCOTT
          You've got that right. He was a member
          of some California biker gang called
          the Vipers. He's a complete dirtbag but

                                        (CONTINUED)

CONTINUED:

                    turned state's evidence regarding
                    murders, weapons and drug dealing.
                    I don't know all the details and I'm
                    not sure how it all played out...it's
                    actually inconceivable...a cop was killed
                    during a jewelry heist he was involved
                    with...but the Feds and the state AG
                    thought the people he gave up were more
                    important. That's how he wound up here
                    in witness protection...three thousand
                    miles away.

                         CHRIS
                      (more intense)
                    He's a cop killer? Captain...please
                    don't tell me he's going to walk.

                         CAPTAIN SCOTT
                    No...he's not going to walk...not
                    for what he did. Besides, after
                    tangling with you he's comatose...
                    feeding intravenously. I've already
                    spoken to the prosecutor's office
                    and the U.S. Attorney. He's going
                    down...big time if he's ever able
                    to face trial. And there's one more
                    thing. That supposed wife of his,
                    Sue Crespa...she's going to testify
                    that she knew what he was doing to
                    Julie Prescott, but was terrified to
                    do or say anything. Supposedly, she
                    hooked up with him in New Jersey and
                    didn't know details of his previous
                    life.

Chris becomes visibly upset at the mention of Julie
Prescott's name. Slowly, he lowers his head and stares at
the floor. This is not lost on Captain Scott.

                                                    (CONTINUED)

CONTINUED:

                    CAPTAIN SCOTT
          I'm not sure how that poor kid
          was placed in that house as a
          foster child. Sometimes the
          system fails miserably.

                    CHRIS
          I'll say.

Captain Scott nods and the two share a few silent moments.
Finally Captain Scott breaks the silence.

                    CAPTAIN SCOTT
          On a brighter note I have some good news
          for you. I've submitted your name for the
          departmental Medal of Honor...twice.

                    CHRIS
          Twice sir?

                    CAPTAIN SCOTT
          Yes...the lake rescue and the fight with
          Crespa, who was flying high on PCP and
          meth. You saved multiple lives while
          risking your own...twice within an
          hour...that's quite unprecedented.

                    CHRIS
          Thank you, sir.

                    CAPTAIN SCOTT
          Between you and me Chris...I've thanked
          the Good Lord you were on duty that day.
          I'm extremely proud of your actions
          and consider you our finest officer.

                    CHRIS
          Thank you, sir. I'm highly honored. And
          I too, have prayed thanks to God to have
          given me the strength to prevail.

The two men shake hands across the desk.

                                        FADE TO BLACK

FADE IN FROM BLACK

INT. POLICE CRUISER - NIGHT

Chris is on routine patrol.

                    POLICE RADIO
          Unit five-one.

                    CHRIS
          Five-one here.

                    POLICE RADIO
          10-70.

Chris hits a button on the radio.

                    CHRIS
          Five-one go.

                    POLICE RADIO
          Five-one...go to 48 Park Drive.
          Domestic dispute. That's Sgt.
          Addison's residence. Backup en
          route from headquarters.

                    CHRIS
          Five-one 10-4...10-71.

Chris frowns a bit.

EXT. DARK STREET - NIGHT

Chris exits his car and approaches the front door of the
residence. A grim-faced woman meets him at the door. She is
MRS. ADDISON.

                    CHRIS
          Good evening, ma'am.

                    MRS. ADDISON
          I wish it was...he's been drinking
          all night. Not the usual nonsense
          though. He threatened to shoot himself.

                                        (CONTINUED)

CONTINUED:

Chris remains impassive.

                    CHRIS
          Where was he when you saw him last?

                    MRS. ADDISON
          In our bedroom...with the lights off.
          End of the hall on the left.

                    CHRIS
          I'm going inside to talk with him.
          I think it's best you stay out here
          and tell my backup what's happening.
          I'd prefer to keep this off the air
          in case Mr. Addison is listening to
          crosstalk on the scanner.

Mrs. Addison nods.

                    MRS. ADDISON
          He's listening all right. And before
          you leave, will you take his gun from
          him, please?

Chris nods and steps into the house.

INT. SGT. ADDISON'S HOUSE

A table lamp illuminates the living room but the hallway
leading towards the bedroom is dark. Chris walks slowly to
the edge of the living room.

                    CHRIS
          Hey Sarge...you back there?

                    SGT. ADDISON (O.S.)
                    (shouting-slurred)
          Who the hell is that?

                                        (CONTINUED)

CONTINUED:

                    CHRIS
          It's Chris Simone

               SGT. ADDISON (O.S.)
                    (angry)
          Get out of my house Simone. You're
          the last person I want to see.

                    CHRIS
          Come on, Sarge. Why don't you come
          out here.

               SGT. ADDISON (O.S.)
                    (bellowing)
          GET OUT!

Chris glances back towards Mrs. Addison standing near the
front door. He waves for her to leave the house and she
does. He turns back towards the hall.

                    CHRIS
          Sarge...I'm going to come in...
          nice and slow...alright?

Chris begins to walk slowly down the hall. As he approaches
the bedroom he can see soft light illuminating within. He
stops at the door frame.

                    CHRIS
          Sarge...why don't you come this way
          so we can talk face to face.

               SGT. ADDISON (O.S.)
                    (threatening)
          I told you to get out Simone. I mean it!

                                        (CONTINUED)

CONTINUED:

Chris peeks inside of the bedroom. Sgt. Addison is standing
near an open closet, a three quarters empty whiskey bottle
on the floor. The light within casts a soft glow. He's in
his underwear and his hair is disheveled. Chris can't see
his hands which are inside the closet.

                         CHRIS
                        (calm)
                 Come on, Sarge...

                    SGT. ADDISON
                     (sobbing)
                 What's the point...of anything?

Chris steps inside of the bedroom. Sgt. Addison looks at
him and steps back, showing he's armed with a handgun.
Chris' face remains impassive.

                    SGT. ADDISON
                 You're not very smart...are you Simone?

Sgt. Addison walks towards Chris while raising the handgun
to his own head. Chris holds his hands out, palms up.

                         CHRIS
                 Please don't do this. You're just
                 having a tough moment. We all have
                 them.

                    SGT. ADDISON
                 Oh really...Mis-ter per-fect Blue
                 Knight?

Sgt. Addison closes his eyes and Chris moves slowly towards
him. Suddenly Addison opens his eyes, sees that Chris has
advanced and points the weapon at him. He cocks the handgun
single action. Chris freezes in place, just out of reach.
Addison's face is suddenly a mask of ghastly exultation.

                                        (CONTINUED)

CONTINUED:

                         SGT. ADDISON
                    Kiss it goodbye, Simone.

Addison pulls the trigger but the handgun just clicks.
Chris moves like a blur, grabbing the gun from Addison's
hand. Addison lunges forward but Chris quickly sidesteps,
drops him with an elbow to the jaw and handcuffs him.

                           CHRIS
                      (deeply troubled)
                  Jesus Christ, Sarge...you really
                  hate me that much?

Addison looks up at Chris with eyes full of tears and
shakes his head.

                         SGT. ADDISON
                  Yeah...but not nearly as much
                  as I hate myself.

Chris pulls Addison to his feet, grabs a bathrobe tossed
across the bed and wraps it around Addison's shoulders. He
walks the man out of the room.

                           CHRIS
                    Let's go.

                                          FADE TO BLACK

FADE IN FROM BLACK

INT. HOSPITAL EMERGENCY ROOM CRISIS UNIT WAITING ROOM

Chris is sitting near a door. As the camera pans back a
sign marked 'CRISIS UNIT' comes into view. Suddenly Captain
Scott in plain clothes enters from outside and approaches
Chris. Chris stands.

                                          (CONTINUED)

CONTINUED:

                    CAPTAIN SCOTT
          Chris...what happened? Are you
          alright?

                    CHRIS
          Sure, Captain. I'm ok. Sgt. Addison
          had a little too much to drink...that's
          all.

                    CAPTAIN SCOTT
          What's this about him and a loaded gun?

Chris nodded and shrugged.

                    CHRIS
          Sure...he had his weapon. He was in
          his own house. But nothing came of it.
          I have it secured in my car.

Captain Scott eyes Chris with profound skepticism.

                    CAPTAIN SCOTT
          Are you sure that's going to be
          your version of events?

Chris nods.

                    CHRIS
          Yes sir.

                    CAPTAIN SCOTT
          You know he's off limits and I can't
          question him while he's inside the
          Crisis Unit?

                    CHRIS
          Yes sir.

Captain Scott continues to eye Chris.

                                        (CONTINUED)

CONTINUED:

                    CAPTAIN SCOTT
          Why would you bring him here if
          he had just a 'little too much
          to drink'?

                    CHRIS
          Well sir, he was having a tough time
          tonight dealing with some personal
          stuff...having a lousy day like we
          all do sometimes...I thought the people
          here could help him the most.

Captain Scott nods.

                    CAPTAIN SCOTT
          You know about obstruction of justice,
          Chris?

                    CHRIS
          Of course, Captain. But I haven't
          told you one thing that's untrue.

                    CAPTAIN SCOTT
          Yeah well...it's what you're NOT
          telling me I'm concerned about.

Captain Scott finally looks away from Chris towards the
CRISIS UNIT entrance.

                    CAPTAIN SCOTT
          After all the times he's hounded
          and insulted you, making your life
          miserable...and you're willing to
          help him?

                    CHRIS
          Captain...you've known me for quite
          some time now and how I operate. Did
          you really expect something different
          tonight?

                                        (CONTINUED)

CONTINUED:

Holding his hand to his forehead and sighing, Captain Scott
finally lightens up.

                    CAPTAIN SCOTT
          No...not at all.

The two men stand there in silence for several long moments
but the tenseness is gone.

                    CAPTAIN SCOTT
          I'll expect your completed report
          before you go home.

                    CHRIS
          Yes sir, you'll have it.

Captain Scott nods and walks away from the waiting area,
leaving Chris standing there by himself.

                                        FADE TO BLACK

FADE IN FROM BLACK

INT. POLICE DEPARTMENT LOCKER ROOM

Chris stands before his locker holding something small,
examining the object closely.

INT. CLOSEUP OF OBJECT CHRIS IS HOLDING

Chris holds an unfired bullet. The primer clearly shows the
distinct impression where it had been struck dead center by
a firing pin.

INT. CLOSEUP OF CHRIS' FACE

Chris clasps his hands together and closes his eyes.

                    CHRIS
          Thank-you, God...thank-you
          Jesus...thank-you both, once
          more.

                                        FADE TO BLACK

FADE IN FROM BLACK

INT. AIRPORT TERMINAL - FLIGHT SECURITY GATE ENTRANCE

Denoting the passage of several years from the previous
scene, a visibly matured Chris stands beside his parents
inside a bustling, colossal airport terminal. The sunlight
streams brilliantly through the ceiling-high windows behind
the trio, highlighting a huge sign which reads:
NEWARK INTERNATIONAL AIRPORT
Chris and his parents are in obvious good spirits. In the
background, a line of people slowly begin to file through
the security gate and ensuing metal detector.

                         CHRIS
              Next stop...San Francisco!

                         ISABELLA
              I can't wait! I've always heard
              it's such a beautiful place.

                         ARTURO
              Why do you think Tony Bennett left
              his heart there?

The three share a small laugh. Chris glances at the
dwindling line at the security gate.

                         CHRIS
              Well...I guess it's time.

                         ARTURO
              I think you're right.

                         ISABELLA
              Thank-you, Chris...for everything.

She hugs Chris and he returns the embrace, kissing her on
the cheek.

                         CHRIS
              I wish I'd done this sooner, Mom.

Arturo pats Chris on the shoulder. Chris turns and gives
him an embrace too.

                                        (CONTINUED)

CONTINUED:

                            CHRIS
            Pop, be sure you take care of Mom,
            especially on those hill trolleys.

                            ARTURO
            (pats Chris lovingly on the cheek)
            I will, son. I will.

Chris' parents walk to the end of the line of their flight
gate. Entering the security checkpoint, they turn and wave
to him. Chris waves back, smiling, and is still there as
they disappear from view.

Above him, a digital flight schedule monitor with flashing
updates is close by. The date **9-11-01** boldly stands out at
the top of the monitor, along with **FLIGHT 93 NOW BOARDING.**

INT. CHRIS' HOUSE - DAY

A visibly concerned Chris tosses his car keys on the table
and flicks on the TV. Immediately there is blaring,
breaking news concerning the attack on the World Trade
Center by hijacked planes. His facial expression grows
darker and darker as he sees that both towers have been
struck and are billowing heavy black smoke. He gasps as the
TV reporter announces that a plane was hijacked from Newark
Airport. As the TV image relays the South Tower collapsing,
Chris is holding his face in his hands, slowly shaking his
head side to side.

                                          FADE TO BLACK

SLOW FADE IN FROM BLACK

EXT. CEMETERY - FUNERAL - DAY
Under dark, threatening skies, beneath an open-sided
funeral tent, a large gathering of people stands behind a
distraught Chris as he stares down watching as two caskets
are slowly lowered into the ground in parallel graves.
Father Armand stands beside Chris, praying aloud in Latin

                                          (CONTINUED)

CONTINUED:

and a police honor guard is at attention nearby. As the
caskets disappear below ground the wind begins to gust, the
branches of the adjacent trees shake and the tent flaps
billow accordingly, as a low murmur from the attendees is
heard in response to the abrupt wind squall. The police
honor guard bagpiper plays Amazing Grace as the attendees
file past Chris, offering their condolences. A much older
looking Sgt. Addison, dressed in plain clothes and using a
walking stick is among those paying their respects to him.

                              SLOW FADE TO BLACK

SLOW FADE IN FROM BLACK

EXT. CITY STREET - LATE AFTERNOON - WINTER

People are scurrying from shop to boutique as a gentle snow
falls. Christmas music emanates from the exterior
loudspeakers of the local music store. The camera catches a
prominently displayed sign, with snow clinging to the
edges, which reads:

WELCOME TO LONG BRANCH, NEW JERSEY-THE FRIENDLY CITY.

A nearby sign flashes:

MERRY CHRISTMAS 2001

A green and white police car moves slowly up the street,
then stops near the intersection marked by the street signs
BRIGHTON AVENUE and SECOND AVENUE, adjacent to the curb
where Tom Burke, wearing snow-covered, dark aviator
sunglasses is standing at the crosswalk of the intersection
waiting to cross, holding a package in one hand and a
walking stick in the other.

INT. POLICE CAR

Chris stops his patrol car and looks at the man waiting to
cross the street. Chris exudes melancholy. He smiles
slightly but it's a sad smile.

CLOSEUP - CHRIS SIMONE'S FACE

Chris chuckles as he thinks of his first meeting with Tom
Burke so many years before.

EXT.- CITY STREET - SUMMER NIGHT (CHRIS SIMONE'S FLASHBACK)

A much younger Officer Simone walks the beat late at night,
long after all the businesses are closed and encounters Tom
Burke for the first time.

EXT. - CITY STREET - PRESENT

He exits the patrol car and approaches Tom waiting on the
corner to cross. Chris now wears sergeant stripes.

                         CHRIS
              Hey...Tom Burke...Merry Christmas to you.

                         TOM
              Buon Natale, Chris! How about this snow?

Chris moves next to Tom and offers him an arm. As if on cue
the blind man touches the officer's elbow, allowing himself
to be guided across the street. Chris holds up his free
hand to stop the slow-moving traffic. In a few moments,
they reach the opposite curb near the bike shop. The
clinging, wet snow quickly covers Chris' black hair. Tom is
wearing a snow-covered ski cap.

                         TOM
                   So, my old friend...you're working
                   today of all days? You've been on
                   the force long enough to have off
                   for Christmas.

                         CHRIS
                   You know me, Tom. Need to keep busy...
                   besides...it's a good time for one
                   of our young guys with kids to stay
                   home and enjoy his family.

                         TOM
              Will you be at midnight mass?

                                        (CONTINUED)

CONTINUED:

                    CHRIS
          I don't know...I'm working till twelve...
          by the time I change out of uniform...

                    TOM
          So...come in uniform.

                    CHRIS
          I don't know...maybe...we'll see.
          Well, I'm going to make my rounds.
          I'll see you later, Tom.

                    TOM
          Okay Chris. Talk to you later.

EXT. DUSK

In the gathering darkness, Chris enters his patrol car and
slowly drives off.

EXT. NIGHT

Chris stops and helps a stranded motorist who had run out
of gas, transporting him to the gas station and back to the
stalled car.

EXT. NIGHT

Chris stops to unlock a car door for a frantic woman with a
baby locked within, who promptly hugs Chris and kisses his
cheek after he opens the door. Chris smiles bashfully and
tips his hat to her.
EXT. NIGHT

Chris stops and provides directions to gift-bearing out-of-
towners who had waved him down, searching for the elusive
street and house number.

INT. PARKED PATROL CAR

Chris is catching up on report writing. Finally, just as
the streets begin to quiet down duty beckons once again.

                    POLICE CAR RADIO
          Car Five-one.

                         CHRIS
                    (reaches for the mic)
          Five-one here.

                    POLICE CAR RADIO
          Car Five-one...ten thirty-nine
          St. Michael's Church...see the
          priest...reference theft.

                         CHRIS
          Five-one...ten-four.

Chris returns the microphone to its bracket. A look that is
at once perplexed and disappointed is etched upon his face
as he contemplates the call, mumbling to himself.

                         CHRIS
                    (incredulous)
          Theft...from a church...on
          Christmas Eve?

EXT. CHURCH - NIGHT

The patrol car approaches St. Michael's Church, a red-
bricked structure with a steeple reaching high into the
snowy night, a lofty alcove highlighted by spotlight,
graced with the statue of the winged Archangel Michael
gazing knowingly upon the world. Outside the front entrance
of the church Father Armand stands beside a life-sized
nativity scene. The patrol car stops so the headlights
illuminate the interior of the crèche. Large, drifting
snowflakes gleam brilliantly through the beams. The priest
steps towards the patrol car. Chris exits the patrol car.

                         CHRIS
          Merry Christmas, Father Armand.
          What happened?

                                             (CONTINUED)

CONTINUED:

                    FATHER ARMAND
               (gesturing inside the crèche)
          Hello, Chris. Would you believe someone
          took the swaddling blanket from the baby
          Jesus? I had just placed Him here after
          sunset mass.

                    CHRIS
          What color's the blanket?

                    FATHER ARMAND
          White with blue trim.

                    CHRIS
          Maybe...someone walking by was cold.

Chris closely examines the life-size figures surrounding
the cradle.

                    CHRIS
          This display is a much different
          than last year's.

                    FATHER ARMAND
          You're very observant...this one's
          hand-carved from Jerusalem olivewood.

                    CHRIS
          Jerusalem, eh?

                    FATHER ARMAND
          Yes...on loan from the Church of
          the Holy Sepulcher. Cut from trees
          grown near Golgotha.

Chris seems entranced by the exceedingly lifelike icons of
faith displayed before him. Mary and Joseph kneeling upon
the straw. The Three Kings stand behind, surrounded by the
kindred creatures of the manger. All of them seem to exude
a forlorn presence while gazing towards the uncovered baby
in the cradle.

                                        (CONTINUED)

CONTINUED:

Chris looks back and forth at the solemn faces of Mary and
Joseph, then slowly lowers his head and stares at the
ground. This does not go unnoticed by Father Armand, who
looks at Chris with an empathetic, knowing eye. He has the
look of someone thinking about another time and place.

                                              DISSOLVE TO:

INT. - CHURCH RECTORY - NIGHT (FATHER ARMAND'S FLASHBACK)

By the light of a solitary floor lamp, Father Armand sits
opposite an obviously distraught Chris, out of police
uniform. Tears stream down his face. On the wall, in the
background is a calendar. Judging from the boldly marked-
off days it is September 24, 2001.

                         FATHER ARMAND
                    It wasn't your fault, Chris. You must
                    not think that way. You had no way of
                    knowing what would happen. How could you?

                         CHRIS
                    (eyes filled with tears)
                    Of course it's my fault. Who bought them
                    the plane tickets? Made the reservations?
                    Of all the times I could have sent them on
                    a vacation they deserved so much, I picked
                    the day...me...no one else...I picked the
                    day to send them to their deaths...

                         FATHER ARMAND
                    Many people died on that awful day...

                         CHRIS
                    (sobbing)
                    Yeah, Father? How many were killed by
                    their son?

                         FATHER ARMAND
                    You didn't kill them, Chris. Terrorists
                    killed them...along with three thousand
                    other innocent people.

                                              (CONTINUED)

CONTINUED:

                    CHRIS
               (increasingly agitated)
          I killed them all right...Instead
          of sending them to visit their
          lifelong dream...San Francisco...
          I sent them out on Nine-Eleven...
          to die in some God-forsaken place
          called SHANKSVILLE!

                    FATHER ARMAND
               (calm)
          Chris...Why don't we take a moment
          to reach out to God...seek His infinite
          wisdom?

                    CHRIS
               (glaring, eyes blazing)
          Reach out to God? Reach out to GOD?
          Where was GOD when my parents' plane
          was hijacked and crashed? Where was
          GOD when my parents were murdered...
          when the Trade Center collapsed
          with all those people inside?

Chris stands and walks abruptly toward the door, still
sobbing but angrier by the moment.

                    CHRIS
          Sell GOD to someone who believes,
          Father. For me... those days are
          over!

                    FATHER ARMAND
               (pleading)
          Please Chris...please...don't leave
          like this.

As the door slams shut Father Armand stands, dejection
etched on his face, looking towards the exit Chris had just
disappeared through as if hoping he'd return. After a long
moment, he glances to the ceiling for an instant before
clasping his hands. Turning, he approaches a crucifix on
the rectory wall, lowering his head.

                                        (CONTINUED)

CONTINUED:

                    FATHER ARMAND
                       (softly)
          Dear Heavenly Father...please forgive
          Chris...he didn't mean what he said...
          he's a lost soul right now...a kind,
          decent, brave man who's lost his way...
          You know he helps people every single
          day above and beyond his calling in life...
          I've tried and tried to reach him, but
          now he needs Your help...please God...
          please help him.

                                        DISSOLVE TO:

EXT. NIGHT- CRECHE - PRESENT

Father Armand nods slightly, thoughtfully.

                    FATHER ARMAND
          Chris?

                    CHRIS
          (snapping out of his trancelike state)
          Yes, Father?

                    FATHER ARMAND
          Whoever took the swaddling blanket was
          Wearing what looked like a white robe.

                    CHRIS
          How do you know?

                    FATHER ARMAND
          One of our parishioners drove by after
          sunset. He told me he saw a man emerge
          from here, thought he was wearing a full-
          length white robe. Said at first, he
          thought it was me then saw he was young,
          with long, dark hair.

                                        (CONTINUED)

CONTINUED:

Chris shines his flashlight upon the ground, illuminating footprints in the new snow leading away from the crèche, up the sidewalk, along the main street towards the shopping area. A brief close-up of these prints reveals they are not the shape of those made by a regular shoe but rather the contour outline of a barefooted person.

                         CHRIS
               I'll follow these prints afterwards,
               Father.

Chris enters the crèche. He notices something white hanging from the top of the cradle. Reaching down he grasps a small strip of white material with blue trim. After examining the piece by flashlight, he places it in a small plastic bag marked **EVIDENCE**.

                    PORTABLE POLICE RADIO
               Car Five-one.

                         CHRIS
                    (keying the lapel mic)
               Five-one here.

                    PORTABLE POLICE RADIO
               Five-one...are you able to break away?

                         CHRIS
               Ten-four to that.

                    PORTABLE POLICE RADIO
               Five-one...see the manager Chowder
               Pot restaurant...reference...non-
               paying customer.

                         CHRIS
               Five-one...ten-four.

Chris turns to the priest.

                                             (CONTINUED)

CONTINUED:

                    CHRIS
          Father, I'll let the other units know
          What happened here. We'll keep our eyes
          open.

                    FATHER ARMAND
          Thank-you, son. Merry Christmas to you.
          Maybe, we'll see you tonight for midnight
          mass?

                    CHRIS
               (clearly uncomfortable)
          Ah...I'm not sure...anyways...Merry
          Christmas, Father.

Chris enters the patrol car and slowly drives off. The
route that he takes parallels the footprints in the snow,
and he's shining the exterior spotlight on the ground,
indicating he's following the trail.

CLOSE-UP FATHER ARMAND'S FACE

The priest is obviously saddened as he watches the patrol
car proceed toward the main road. After a long moment, he
turns, first glancing into the darkened crèche, then
proceeding towards the church.

EXT. PARKING LOT -NIGHT

Chris parks the patrol car near the entrance of the CHOWDER
POT restaurant. The parking lot is filled with snow-covered
cars. Chris glances up at the restaurant's red neon sign
and enters through the front door.

INT. - DINING ROOM ENTRANCE

Chris scans the packed dining room. Several patrons look
towards him with curious expressions. A waitress waves to
Chris, gesturing him toward a table where a man
with an annoyed, pompous manner stands. He has a sparse,
uneven moustache with matching hair that resembles that of
a store mannequin's. His name is RICHARD, and he is the
assistant manager of the CHOWDER POT.

                                        (CONTINUED)

CONTINUED:

                    RICHARD
              (snapping his fingers)
          Here, Officer.

Chris walks to the table, his expression more impassive
than usual, pretending that the finger snapping didn't
bother him. As he reaches the table he sees the hub of the
commotion: a young man sitting there with his hands folded
on the tabletop. A sad smile adorns the man's bearded,
ruddy face, his shoulder-length hair tucked behind his
ears. He appears to be uncomfortable, unaccustomed to this
type of negative attention.

                    RICHARD
                   (acerbic)
          If he's not going to pay, Officer,
          I want him arrested.

                    CHRIS
          How about we talk inside so the folks
          in this room can enjoy their dinner?

Chris gestures to the young man sitting at the table.

                    CHRIS
          Why don't you come with me, sir.

The man complies, stands slowly, walks out of the dining
room with Chris following close behind. Chris observes the
man is barefooted.

INT. CHOWDER POT WAITING ROOM

Chris looks the man up and down, noting he is wrapped in a
long, white blanket with blue trim and is about as tall as
Father Armand. His name is JEDIDIAH.

                    CHRIS
          What's your name?

                                              (CONTINUED)

CONTINUED:

                    JEDIDIAH
                 (voice gentle)
          My name is Jedidiah. I offered to
          work in exchange for food, but the
          manager refused.

                    CHRIS
          What did you order?

                    JEDIDIAH
          Grilled sole and scallions...with
          a glass of water.

                    CHRIS
                 (Mildly amused)
          Grilled sole and scallions? Why
          didn't you go to the burger joint
          up the street? You could have had
          eaten more food there for less money.

                    JEDIDIAH
          There...you must pay for your food
          before eating.

                    CHRIS
                 (expression softening)
          You have no money?

                    JEDIDIAH
          No...I don't. In the past I've always
          managed to work for the cost of my
          food. Not tonight...I guess.

At that moment, Richard enters the waiting room with the
pretty waitress who had served Jedidiah his dinner. She
looks to be of college student age and smiles at Chris
before nervously flicking her eyes toward Richard and
looking away.

                                        (CONTINUED)

CONTINUED:

                         RICHARD
                    (harsh, glaring)
          I can't believe you served someone
          who's barefooted...wrapped in a blanket!

The waitress casts her eyes to the floor, humiliated.
Richard turns towards Chris.

                         RICHARD
          So Officer, is the man going to pay
          or what?

                         CHRIS
          How much does he owe?

                         RICHARD
          Eleven dollars and forty-three cents.

                         CHRIS
          Well then...eleven forty-three it is.

Chris reaches into his pocket, peals a twenty-dollar bill
from his money clip and hands it to the WAITRESS.

                         CHRIS
          Tip included.

                         WAITRESS
                    (beaming)
          You're one of those nice policemen.

                         CHRIS
          Well...I don't know about that...but
          it is Christmas.

                         RICHARD
                    (pouting, perturbed)
          Wait one minute! If he doesn't pay,
          you're supposed to arrest him...not
          pay for his meal. If the word gets
          out about this, we'll be overrun by
          his kind.

                                            (CONTINUED)

CONTINUED:

                    CHRIS
          I'll talk to him after we leave...
          you may rest assured he won't come
          back.

                    RICHARD
          That's totally unacceptable.

                    CHRIS
          (trying hard not to show annoyance)
          The meal's paid for...why don't we just
          call it a night and everyone have a Merry
          Christmas?

                    RICHARD
          NOOO...

As he emphasizes the word his moustache twitches.

                    RICHARD
          I must INSIST on you doing your job,
          Officer. Give the policeman his
          money back.

The waitress looks to Chris for help. Chris steps in front
of Richard, making direct eye contact with him.

                    CHRIS
          Listen...I'm not arresting this man
          for being hungry. The meal's paid for.
          Why don't you let it drop?

There is murmuring from the dining room as the patrons are
craning to get a look at their local police in action.

                    RICHARD
          (louder, more obnoxious)
          Absolutely not...if you were doing
          your job, there'd be no need to have
          this conversation.

                    CHRIS
          I'm not arresting this man. If you
          wish to pursue this you can stop by
          the municipal court on Wednesday.

Chris takes Jedidiah by the elbow and guides him towards
the exit.

                    CHRIS
          Come on, Jedidiah.

                    RICHARD
              (infuriated, flustered)
          You're supposed to be serving the
          taxpayers of this town...not penniless
          losers...I know your chief...I'll have
          your badge for this!

People in the dining room begin to chuckle at Richard. One
man calls out, asking him where his heart is. Chris glances
at the still-smiling Jedidiah and nudges him through the
exit. He turns back towards Richard with a cold eye.

                    CHRIS
          I know the chief too and if you can
          'have my badge' for something like
          this...then it was never worth having
          in the first place.

Chris exits behind Jedidiah and the door slams shut.

EXT. SNOW COVERED PARKING LOT - NIGHT

The quiet solitude of the windless winter night quickly
envelopes the two men. The snowflakes are larger than
before and fall without pause. The dark hair of both men is
quickly covered by white. They approach the patrol car,
Chris eyeing Jedidiah up and down.

                    CHRIS
          Jedidiah, I need to pat you down
          before you get into the car with me.

                                        (CONTINUED)

CONTINUED:

                    JEDIDIAH
                (raises his arms)
          Of course...I understand.

Chris pats him down, encountering naught. By his expression
he does notice that Jedidiah is wearing next to nothing
under the blanket.

                    CHRIS
          Where are the rest of your clothes?

                    JEDIDIAH
          For now, this is all I have.

                    CHRIS
          Aren't you cold?

                    JEDIDIAH
          Yes, a bit.

Chris shines his flashlight upon Jedidiah's makeshift
sleeves. He notices that one is torn, and there is a strand
of straw clinging to the other. Sweeping the light beam, he
discovers Jedidiah's newly created footprints in the snow
seem to match the size of those at the nativity scene.

                    CHRIS
                (frowning)
          Were you near the church earlier?

                    JEDIDIAH
          The church?

                    CHRIS
          Yes...the big red church three blocks
          from here? The one...with the nativity
          scene? The crèche?

                    JEDIDIAH
                (nods with the word 'crèche')
          Yes, I was there before.

                                        (CONTINUED)

CONTINUED:

                    CHRIS
               (eyeing JEDIDIAH closely)
          Someone took the blanket from the baby
          Jesus there...do you know anything about
          that?

                    JEDIDIAH
               (unflinchingly)
          I was cold...I did take the blanket...
          but I shall return it later.

                    CHRIS
          You just appeared at the church...naked
          ...and borrowed a blanket from the crèche?

                    JEDIDIAH
          Yes...I wouldn't lie to you.

                    CHRIS
          I've been a cop for twenty-two years...
          I'm good at telling when someone's lying
          to me. I don't know why...

Chris slowly nods his head.

                    CHRIS
          But I guess you're not...at least...
          I believe you're telling me your
          version of the truth.

Chris opens the back door of the patrol car, gestures for
Jedidiah to enter. Jedidiah sits down. Chris speaks to him
thru the opened car door.

                    CHRIS
          So...where do you live?

                    JEDIDIAH
          I...don't really stay in one place.

                                             (CONTINUED)

CONTINUED:

                    CHRIS
          Where are you from?

                  JEDIDIAH
          I'm...originally from Bethlehem...

                    CHRIS
          No kidding? You're definitely a long
          way from home. I had an uncle who
          worked there back in the day...in a
          steel mill right on the banks of the
          Delaware.

Jedidiah smiles but says nothing. Chris removes a roll of
wintergreen Lifesavers from his pocket, pops one in his
mouth, then offers the candy to Jedidiah, who looks at the
roll with uncertainty before gingerly taking one. After a
few moments his eyes open wide.

                  JEDIDIAH
          These are quite tasty.

                    CHRIS
          Haven't you had a Lifesaver before?

                  JEDIDIAH
          A what?

                    CHRIS
          A Lifesaver.

                  JEDIDIAH
          No...I haven't.

Chris studies Jedidiah's face in a manner to suggest the
man is putting him on but he detects naught. Shaking his
head, he closes the back door of the patrol car and climbs
into the driver's seat.

INT. - PATROL CAR

Chris glances into the rear-view mirror and sees Jedidiah
looking back at him.

                    CHRIS
          Well, Jedidiah, I can't very well drop
          you off on a snowy street wearing just
          a blanket and say 'Good Night'. Where
          are you staying for Christmas?

                    JEDIDIAH
           I'm...not staying anywhere.

                    CHRIS
          The shift commander won't want you at
          headquarters. I could try calling the
          welfare director...but she won't be
          easy to contact on Christmas Eve. But
          don't worry, we'll find you a place.

                    JEDIDIAH
          Your generosity and concern is appreciated
          ...but actually Chris...I'm here for you.

                    CHRIS
                    (perplexed)
          You're here for me? How'd you know my first
          name?

                    JEDIDIAH
          I was sent here tonight...to guard your life.

                    CHRIS
          What was that?

                    JEDIDIAH
          I was sent here tonight to guard your life.

                    CHRIS
          You were sent here to guard my life? Sent
          here by whom?

                    JEDIDIAH
          I was sent here at your parents' request.

                                        (CONTINUED)

CONTINUED:

                    CHRIS
          (turns slowly, deliberately)
     What did you say about my parents?

                    JEDIDIAH
     Your parents asked God to guard your life...
     tonight...and He has sent me to do just that.

                    CHRIS
          (anger welling)
     Now wait just one minute...how do you
     know about me? About my parents? Did
     one of those idiots from my squad put
     you up to this? Talk about CROSSING
     THE LINE!

Chris is uncharacteristically seething with anger,
involuntarily grating his teeth. Suddenly the police radio
blares with an excited dispatcher's voice.

                    POLICE CAR RADIO
     Five-one! Five-one and any units near
     Elberon Avenue...Ten-Nineteen...active
     Ten-Nineteen...twenty-two Elberon Avenue
     ...That's two-two Elberon Avenue...Fire
     Department dispatched!

Chris punches the car pedal to the floor.

                    CHRIS
     Five-one en route...e.t.a. one minute.
          (calls over his shoulder)
     Jedidiah...I'm the closest one to the
     fire...just sit tight and we'll take
     care of you later.

Chris glances in the rearview mirror and sees Jedidiah's
eyes glint a lambent jade through the dimness of the patrol
car. Chris frowns and shrugs as the patrol car's overhead
lights flash and the siren yelps through the quiet streets.

EXT. POLICE CAR - NIGHT

With lights and siren activated, the patrol car races through the snowy, deserted streets, passing St. Michael's Church while en route to the fire scene.

EXT. WIDE ANGLE VIEW OF THE FIRE - NIGHT

Through bare tree branches from a vantage point across Takanassee Lake, flames are seen shooting out of the windows of a huge Victorian house. The police car moves swiftly across a bridge and turns up the street toward the fire. The siren fades as the patrol car disappears from view.

INT. PATROL CAR

                    CHRIS
          Five-one is ten-nine. We have a working
          house fire...have the fire department
          expedite!
                    (turns for a moment)
          You just sit tight, Jedidiah.

EXT. - PATROL CAR - NIGHT

Chris jumps out of the car, grabs a CO2 extinguisher from the trunk and eyes the raging fire with grim intensity. He runs up to a group of people gathered around a woman holding a baby with two small children huddled against her robe. Seeing Chris, the woman gestures towards the burning house.

                    WOMAN
               (shrieking hysterically)
          I can't find my son! I can't find
          my Ricky!

                    CHRIS
          Do you think he's still inside?

                    WOMAN
          They were playing hide and seek. He
          must still be in there!

                                        (CONTINUED)

CONTINUED:

> CHRIS
> I'm going in...don't worry Mom...
> I'll find him.

Fire Department truck sirens sound from far off in the distance.

EXT. BURNING HOUSE - SIDE DOOR

Chris hurries through a side door away from the shooting flames and enters the house.

INT. BURNING HOUSE

Chris encounters dense smoke. Coughing, he ducks down, feeling his way, flashlight in one hand, fire extinguisher in the other. The smoke alarm and crackle of flames is loud.

> CHRIS
> (shouting)
> Ricky! Ricky!

Chris continues to crawl along the floor, keeping his head near the ground, opening closet doors. He pulls open a door and sees a long flight of stairs leading down.

> CHRIS
> (shouting)
> Ricky!

There is comparatively little smoke in the staircase, so Chris crawls in for a breather.

INT. STAIRCASE LEADING TO CELLAR

Gulping for air he is about to head back into the main floor of the house when he sees a small figure crouched against the bottom of the staircase. Chris drops the extinguisher and grabs at the small boy, pulling him along. This is RICKY.

(CONTINUED)

CONTINUED:

                         CHRIS
            Come on, buddy. Let's get out of here.

                         RICKY
                   (resisting, cries out)
            Pepe's under the stairs!

                         CHRIS
            Pepe?

                         RICKY
            My cat!

Chris shines his flashlight under the crawlspace beneath
the staircase.

INT. CRAWLSPACE BENEATH THE STAIRCASE

Two yellow eyes reflect in the flashlight beam.

INT. CELLAR - BOTTOM OF STAIRCASE

                         CHRIS
                      (grimacing)
            Just great!

Chris reaches in and grabs the cat. The young feline is
terrified and doesn't resist. Chris sweeps the child and
the cat in his arms and leaps up the stairs. No sooner does
he reach the top landing when the hallway ceiling
collapses, trapping them in the cellar. Chris darts back
down the stairs.

INT. CELLAR

Chris frantically searches for a door or a window. The
walls are aligned ceiling to floor with shelving, covered
with mason jars of canned fruit and vegetables. The cellar
is rapidly filling with smoke.

                         CHRIS
            Where's the door that leads outside?

                                              (CONTINUED)

CONTINUED:

                         RICKY
            This is a cold cellar...that's the only
            door!

Ricky points to the blocked stairs they just descended.
Chris keeps moving along, finally finding a tiny brick-
lined window the size of an air vent. He puts Ricky down
and hands Pepe to him, then pulls on the latch, which
doesn't budge from years of non-use. With a forehand swat
he smashes the glass with his flashlight and tugs the
frame open. They are below a small window well beneath
bushes hugging the house. Chris eyes the opening in a
manner to suggest he knows there is no possible way he will
fit through.

                         CHRIS
            Listen Ricky...you and Pepe climb out first.

                         RICKY
            I'm scared!

                         CHRIS
            It's alright. Once you're outside...
            get away from the house! Tell the fire
            fighters I'm down here...ok? Go ahead now.

Chris removes his coat and places it over the broken frame
and glass, pushing first the child, who squeezes through
the snug window without much room to spare and then the
cat. He watches them disappear through the window frame,
less than one-foot square.

Chris finds an old storage chest and drags it beneath the
window. He gasps as the smoke is choking him now. He steps
upon the chest and gulps what little fresh air he can from
the opening. Keying his lapel mic he tries to speak but
coughs heavily instead, the radio sounding static and
nothing else. He shines his flashlight back and forth
through the window, trying to gain attention.

EXT. REAR GROUND LEVEL VIEW OF BURNING HOUSE

A lonely sight, Chris' flashlight beam is the only movement
visible from the ground level rear of the burning house.
As the camera view pans higher it is obvious that all the
activity is concentrated in the front on the street as the
fire department establishes presence in the midst of noisy,
semi-controlled chaos. Heavily equipped fire fighters try
to gain access but are beaten back by searing flames
curling up like huge, writhing, fiery claws, especially the
side door Chris initially entered.

EXT. STREET - FRONT OF BURNING HOUSE

Ricky's mother wails with relief as she is reunited with
her son, who in turn is cradling Pepe in his arms. They are
surrounded by a smiling, mixed crowd of neighbors, fire
fighters and police officers. Ricky pushes himself free of
his mother's grasp and turns to the police and fire
fighters and points to the house

                         RICKY
               There's a policeman trapped in there...
               he can't get out!

                         POLICE OFFICER
                    (hands on Ricky's shoulders)
               Where, son...where?

                         RICKY
               He's trapped in the cold cellar...there's
               only one tiny window leading to the
               backyard...it was tight for me...he can't
               possibly fit! You gotta help him!

The men exchange brief, frantic looks then take off running
towards the backyard. In the background, nearly lost in all
the commotion, is a view of Chris' patrol car. The overhead
lights are still flashing, but one of the backdoors is
ajar, revealing the darkened interior, illuminated by the
external light emanating from other emergency vehicles. As
the camera pans in, it is obvious the car is unoccupied.

EXT. BACKYARD - BURNING HOUSE

The police officers and fire fighters frantically search
for the elusive cold cellar window, but by now the house is
engulfed in flames. Burning debris has fallen upon the
bushes behind which lies the cold cellar window. The men
finally converge in their hopelessness. One of the police
officers covers his face with his hands, while the other,
Joe O'Connor begins to cry aloud, dropping to his knees,
facing the burning house.

                    JOE O'CONNOR
                 (crying, bellowing)
           CHRIS! CHRIS!

INT. CELLAR

Chris is slumped beneath the window, on the verge of
unconsciousness. Besides his face, all that is visible is
the thick smoke swirling through his flashlight beam. The
ceiling above the staircase suddenly crashes down, and a
broken piece of the supporting floor beam strikes Chris a
glancing blow on his head. Intense fire is closing fast.

CLOSEUP - CHRIS' FACE

Chris, illuminated by his flashlight beam, appears resigned
to his fate. Suddenly, he looks up.

INT. CELLAR

Barely visible through the darkness and the smoke, a
solitary figure stands over Chris. The figure bends down
and draws close. It is Jedidiah. His eyes shimmer as they
had in the patrol car. Chris tries to warn him to get out
but can't speak.

Jedidiah's gentle voice blots out all other sound.

                    JEDIDIAH
           God didn't save you from a monster and
           a bullet to let you to die here tonight.

Jedidiah places a hand upon Chris' chest. A glimmer of
light seems to pass between the two men. At once Chris'
eyes open wide, his face taking on new life.

EXT. NIGHT SKY

The snow-covered world floats slowly below Chris'
consciousness as a sensation of flying evolves into a
whirling montage of significant memories from Chris' past:

INT. HOSPITAL ROOM - NIGHT

Chris as a small boy on the hospital bed, perilously sick,
his mother beside him, caring for him.

EXT. GLEAMING OMNIPOTENT RADIANCE

The beautiful angel moving in close and kissing Chris'
forehead.

EXT. LITTLE LEAGUE BASEBALL GAME

Chris hitting a game winning home run over the center field
fence, swarmed by his teammates after he crosses home
plate, his father hoisting him up as Chris smiles skyward.

EXT. FROZEN LAKE - DAYLIGHT

Chris as a youngster learning how to ice skate with his
father. The pair have the lake to themselves, laughing and
obviously enjoying one another's company. Beyond the lake,
snow covers the ground and trees as far as the eye can see.

INT. POLICE ACADEMY AUDITORIUM

Chris marching with his police academy graduating class,
his parents standing together, proudly marking his
achievement.

INT. APARTMENT LIVING ROOM FLOOR - DAY

Chris and Officer Joe O'Connor offer comfort to Lavanya
while delivering her baby as a blizzard rages outside the
living room window.

EXT. SEMI-FROZEN POND - DAYLIGHT

The same pond where Chris learned to ice skate with his
father is observed once more - this time the scene where he
saved the elderly man and woman from icy drowning deaths.

INT. AIRPORT TERMINAL - FLIGHT SECURITY GATE ENTRANCE

Chris stands beside his parents inside a bustling, colossal airport terminal. The sunlight streams brilliantly through the ceiling-high windows behind the trio, highlighting a huge sign which reads:

NEWARK INTERNATIONAL AIRPORT

In the background, a line of people slowly files through the security gate and ensuing metal detector. A digital flight schedule monitor with flashing updates is close by. The date **9-11-01** boldly stands out at the top of the monitor.

Chris' parents walk to the end of the line of their flight gate. Entering the security checkpoint, they turn and wave to him. Chris waves back, smiling, and is still there as they disappear from view.

EXT. CEMETERY - FUNERAL - DAY

Under dark, threatening skies, beneath an open-sided funeral tent, a large gathering of people stands behind a distraught Chris as he stares down, watching as two caskets are lowered slowly into the ground in parallel graves. Father Armand stands beside Chris, praying aloud in Latin as a police honor guard is at attention nearby. As the caskets disappear from view, the wind begins to gust, the branches of the adjacent trees shake and the tent flaps billow accordingly, as a low clamor from the attendees is heard in response to the abrupt wind squall.

EXT. GRASSY HILLTOP - DAY

Chris' mother and father together arm in arm, expressions at once serene and at peace, standing upon a gently sloping hilltop overlooking a valley, extending far as the eye can see, carpeted with a myriad of beautiful flowers. Angelic resonance sounds, omnipotent as the brilliant sunshine.

EXT. GRASSY HILLTOP - DAY

Jake and Julie Prescott walk hand in hand upon another
gently sloping hilltop overlooking another valley extending
far as the eye can see, carpeted with a myriad of beautiful
flowers. Angelic resonance sounds, omnipotent as the
brilliant sunshine as they both smile in joyful fashion.

                                        DISSOLVE TO:

EXT. NIGHT SKY

The view is from Chris' vantage as he lies upon the ground,
looking up at the silhouette of Jedidiah looking down upon
him. Behind Jedidiah's head the moon is a frosty, luminous
halo peeking through fast-moving clouds. Suddenly,
everything whirls into a darkening vortex.

                                        FADE TO BLACK

FADE IN FROM BLACK

EXT. NIGHT - CLOSEUP OF CHRIS' FACE

Chris is prostrate upon a first aid stretcher, an oxygen
mask on his face. His eyes flick open as he hears voices.

                    JOE O'CONNOR (V.O.)
               He's coming around!

                         CHRIS
               (pulls the mask from his face)
               What's going on? How'd I get out?

EXT. NIGHT

Chris is surrounded by police officers and fire fighters.

                         JOE O'CONNOR
               Good question. You must have squeezed
               through that cellar window...somehow...
               before the main floor collapsed.
               We thought we lost you, Chris. We

                                        (CONTINUED)

CONTINUED:

                  couldn't find you...thought you were
                  trapped inside...then suddenly you
                  were out here on the snow.

Chris begins to sit up but ten hands gently push at him to
remain down.

                        JOE O'CONNOR
                  You're going to the hospital...get
                  yourself checked out...you know...
                  for smoke inhalation.

                        CHRIS
                     (bewildered)
                  But...I was choking...there was no
                  air! Ask Jedidiah...He'll tell you.

The police and firefighters exchange glances

                        JOE O'CONNOR
                  Who's Jedidiah?

                        CHRIS
                  He's the man in my patrol car...from
                  the Chowder Pot. I was giving him a ride
                  when the call came. I told him not to get
                  out of the car...though I don't know how
                  he did 'cause I locked him inside.

Chris eyes the concerned faces listening to him babble
away.

                        CHRIS
                  I remember him standing over me...
                  he told me earlier God had sent him
                  at my parents' request...then I don't
                  remember anything...but I'm telling you...
                  I was dying...the window was too small
                  for me to climb through!

The group exchanges vexed glances before one finally
speaks.

                                                    (CONTINUED)

CONTINUED:

                         JOE O'CONNOR
              Yeah...sure, Chris. Well anyway...
              let's get you to the hospital.

INT. HOSPITAL EMERGENCY ROOM

Chris is resting in the ER, which is quiet due to the
holiday. The expression on his soot-laden face shows he's
preoccupied with thought. Glancing around the ER he does a
retake, seeing a nurse he literally can't take his eyes
off. She is quite stunning, angel like. Suddenly the look
of recognition crosses Chris' face.

EXT. GLEAMING OMNIPOTENT RADIANCE (CHRIS' BOYHOOD FLASHBACK)

Intense light manifests and in the midst of it all a new
figure appears: a beautiful, alluring woman, with
shimmering hair of gold, eyes blue as the Nordic sky at
sunset, skin fair and smooth as porcelain. Smiling,
dazzling, she reaches towards Chris, caressingly kissing
his forehead. The woman is an ANGEL.

INT. HOSPITAL ER

A close-up of the ER nurse as she makes her rounds. Though
not swathed in gleaming radiance, her lustrous blonde hair
pulled back in a French braid, wearing blue scrubs, the
nurse is quite beautiful. She does in fact, possess the
same beauty from Chris' dream, the angel who had visited
him as he lay delirious in the hospital as a small child.

The nurse approaches Chris' bed to check his chart. She
smiles at him. He can't take his eyes off her. Her nametag
says SARA.

                         SARA
              So...how are you feeling?

                                              (CONTINUED)

CONTINUED:

                         CHRIS
                  (at a loss for words)
          I...umm...I'm feeling much better now.

                         SARA
          I'm glad to hear that. I heard you saved
          a little boy from a house fire.

Chris nods a bit.

                         SARA
          You should feel very proud.

                         CHRIS
          I'm just glad the kid's alright.

There's a silence but it's not awkward. Chris and Sara
exchange glances as an attraction seems to develop between
the two.

                         CHRIS
          Your name is Sara?

                         SARA
          Yes.

                         CHRIS
          My name's Chris...Chris Simone.

                         SARA
                  (smiling, taps the clipboard)
          I know.

                         CHRIS
          My mom was a nurse.

                         SARA
                  (interested)
          Really?

                                              (CONTINUED)

CONTINUED:

                    CHRIS
          Absolutely...she worked in this very
          hospital...a long time ago. Listen...
          Sara. I know you probably fend off
          every cop who comes in here...but I'd
          really like to see you again...need to
          see you again.

                    SARA
          (hesitant but obviously interested)
          I don't know.

                    CHRIS
          Look how the fates brought us together...
          on Christmas...besides...this isn't the
          first time I've seen you.

                    SARA
                 (intrigued)
          It's not?

                    CHRIS
                 (serious)
          No...it's not. When I was a young boy...in
          this very hospital...on the edge of death...
          in the dark...afraid...an angel appeared to
          me...a beautiful angel...she took away my
          fear...took away the sickness...
                 (eyes fill with tears)
          and as God is my witness...that angel was you.

A solitary tear streams down Chris' sooty cheek. Sara
blinks back her own tears, visibly moved by Chris' soulful
confession.

                    SARA
          Those are the nicest words anyone's
          ever said to me...
             (hesitates, gathering thought)
          Looks like the doctor's going to release
          you soon...I get off at 8.

                                        (CONTINUED)

CONTINUED:

                    CHRIS
                 (smiling)
          I'm looking forward to 8.

                    SARA
          Me too...you know what else I'm looking
          forward to?

                    CHRIS
          Tell me.

                    SARA
                 (winks at Chris, impish)
          Seeing your face...without the chimney-sweep
          look.

Chris beams at Sara, then gently touches her wrist.

                    CHRIS
          Thank-you...Sara...for everything.

Sara touches Chris' hand that's touching her wrist.

                    SARA
          Until later.

                                        FADE TO BLACK

FADE IN FROM BLACK

EXT. HOUSE FIRE SCENE - NIGHT

Chris is gazing at the roped-off, gutted frame starkly
illuminated by floodlights. A solitary fire truck remains
along with a handful of fire fighters who douse smoldering
embers with water. Chris suddenly turns away and begins
searching the ground. There's a myriad of countless
footprints nearby. Chris moves in the direction from where
he had originally responded to the fire, then stops.
Removing a small flashlight from his pocket, he shines the
beam on the ground before him.

EXT. SNOW COVERED GROUND - NIGHT

The flashlight beam illuminates a set of footprints leading
off alone. Though the fallen snow had obscured them a bit,
they obviously have the same barefoot shape as those made
by Jedidiah which Chris had observed earlier. He begins to
follow the tracks through the streets.

EXT. BRIDGE CROSSING LAKE TAKANASSEE - NIGHT

Chris continues to follow the footprints, his flashlight
illuminating the ground before him.

EXT. ST. MICHAEL'S CHURCH - NIGHT

Chris approaches the church. He notices someone standing on
the walkway, gazing toward the streetlight and its golden
aura filled with countless flakes of gently falling snow.
As he draws near he sees that the person is Tom Burke, who
is clutching his aviator shades instead of wearing them.
Chris gently approaches from behind.

                    CHRIS
          Tom...what is it?

Tom turns towards Chris, teeming with emotion.

                    TOM
          Chris? I can see!

Chris notices the man's eyes.

EXT. CLOSEUP TOM BURKE'S FACE - NIGHT

Illuminated by the streetlight, the man's eyes are full of
sparkle and life, no longer sightless to be hidden away
behind shades. Tom doesn't wait for Chris' follow-up
question.

                    TOM
          A man approached me...He touched my
          face...and I could see.

EXT. ST. MICHAEL'S CHURCH - NIGHT

Tom Burke gestures toward the crèche.

                    TOM
          Then...he went in there.

Chris notices the footprints he's been tracking disappear
inside the crèche.

INT. CRECHE - NIGHT

Approaching slowly, hesitantly, in a manner to suggest he
expects to find someone within, Chris' flashlight beam
discloses naught until he looks inside the cradle.

INT. CRECHE - CLOSEUP OF THE CRADLE

The blanket of baby Jesus has been returned, pristine and
unscorched. The infant is now swaddled in the blanket of
white cloth with blue trim which had been worn by Jedidiah.

INT. CRECHE - NIGHT

By the light of his flashlight, Chris looks at the faces of
Mary and Joseph. The faces are forlorn no longer but serene
now that all is as it should be. Chris searches the shadows
once more. Finally, Chris turns to the cradle.

INT. CRECHE - CLOSEUP OF BABY JESUS IN CRADLE

The baby's kind, gentle face appears to be looking up
toward Chris.

INT. CRECHE

Chris kneels before the cradle, lowering his head into his
hands.

EXT. GRASSY HILLTOP - DAY (FLASHBACK)

Chris' mother and father embraced together, expressions at
once serene and at peace, upon a hilltop overlooking a
valley carpeted with a myriad of beautiful flowers. Angelic
resonance sounds aloud, omnipotent as the brilliant
sunshine.

INT. CRECHE - NIGHT

Chris raises his head from his hands, crosses himself, then
reaches into the cradle and gently touches the blanket
covering the baby Jesus. Smiling slightly, he stands and
walks toward the exit.

EXT. CRECHE - NIGHT

Chris exits the crèche and approaches Tom. He gestures
towards the church.

                         CHRIS
             I missed mass earlier...care to join me?

Tom turns toward the church.

EXT. ST. MICHAEL'S CHURCH - NIGHT

The towering, red-bricked structure, its steeple reaching
high into the snowy night; the cross at rest atop the
spire; a lofty alcove highlighted by spotlight, securing
the statute of the winged Archangel Michael as he gazes
knowingly upon the world. Certainly, wondrous sights for a
blind man to regain his lost vision upon.

EXT. CRECHE - NIGHT

Tom nods to Chris and answers his question.

                         TOM
             Yes...I'll join you.

The two men embrace as dear friends would. After a few
moments they climb the steps and enter the church.

                                        FADE TO BLACK

FADE IN FROM BLACK

EXT. DESERTED BOARDWALK - DAY

The deserted, snow-covered boardwalk extends to the

                                        (CONTINUED)

CONTINUED:

horizon, parallel to the gray, choppy ocean. Chris and Sara
stroll into the scene, each sipping a cup of hot chocolate,
walking closely together. Stopping, they quickly build a
small snowman. They share a laugh, then Chris takes Sara's
hands into his and pulls her close.

EXT. CLOSEUP OF CHRIS AND SARA- DAY

Chris and Sara gaze into one another's eyes.

                         CHRIS
              Tutto quanto puo contenere l'amore
              si puo dire con un bacio.

                         SARA
                   (smiles demurely)
              What did you say to me?

                         CHRIS
              I said, 'Everything that love means
              can be expressed with a kiss.'

Chris kisses Sara, a long, passionate kiss.

                                        FADE TO BLACK

FADE IN FROM BLACK

EXT. ST. MICHAEL'S CHURCH - DAY - SPRING

A smiling Sara and Chris emerge from the church, dressed
respectively as a bride in a white gown and a tuxedoed
groom surrounded by a throng of joyous well-wishers as the
wedding march plays in the background. The couple enters a
waiting limousine, which drives off slowly with Chris and
Sara waving to the crowd.

                       NARRATOR (V.O.)
              Following the Christmas they met,
              Chris proposed to Sara on St. Valentine's
              Day, and they were wed as the spring
              flowers bloomed.

EXT. ST. MICHAEL'S CHURCH - DAY

Father Armand stands with Tom Burke at the top of the
church steps. Both are smiling as they watch Chris and Sara
drive off in the limo.

                    NARRATOR (V.O.)
          Father Armand considered his heavenly
          prayers answered when Sara entered Chris
          Simone's life, and he was called upon to
          officiate the couple's wedding vows at St.
          Michael's Church. Tom Burke accepted the
          honor of being Chris' best man, an honor
          he would cherish as much as knowing that
          the burden Chris had carried for so long
          upon his shoulders had been lifted, replaced
          by a restored faith in God and a new-found
          love.

INT. POLICE DEPARTMENT AWARDS CEREMONY

Before an SRO crowd, Chris, in dress uniform, now wearing
lieutenant's bars, accepts a meritorious decoration from
his police chief and the city's mayor and council. As the
medallion is placed around Chris' neck, the crowd breaks
into a thunderous ovation. A tearful, obviously pregnant
Sara is in front row attendance.

                    NARRATOR (V.O.)
          Lieutenant Chris Simone was ceremoniously
          awarded with the Long Branch Police
          Department's Medal of Honor for the third
          time after selflessly risking his life on
          Christmas Eve of 2001 to save a young child
          from a devastating house fire. The official
          police investigation concluded that despite
          being trapped, his escape route repeatedly
          blocked by lethal flame and smoke, Chris had
          finally managed to rescue the child before
          climbing out a cellar window to safety before
          the house had collapsed upon its foundation.

EXT. LAKESIDE - ADJACENT TO ST. MICHAEL'S CHURCH - DAY

Chris and Sara behind a baby stroller, the baby wearing a
pink bow in her hair the same hue as Sara's, walking around
serene Takanassee Lake as a pair of white swans and a
family of ducks swam close by on a sunny, spring day. As
they pass the church, Chris glances over for an extended
moment, to the area outside the front entrance where the
crèche had once stood. Sara notices Chris' preoccupation
and after a few moments she kisses his cheek.

                    NARRARATOR (V.O.)
          Though his faith was restored and life
          transformed, for Chris Simone, questions
          remained, unanswered:

INT. HOUSE FIRE - CELLAR (FLASHBACK)

Chris near death on the cellar floor. Suddenly, a dark
figure stands over him.

                    NARRATOR (V.O.)
          How did Chris really escape the house fire?

EXT. STREET IFO ST. MICHAEL'S CHURCH - NIGHT FLASHBACK)

A set of bare feet is seen walking through the snow. As the
camera pans upward Jedidiah is striding, alone, away from
the church on Christmas Eve.

                    NARRARATOR (V.O.)
          Who really was Jedidiah, and what
          became of him?

EXT. CHOWDER POT PARKING LOT - NIGHT (FLASHBACK)

Jedidiah sitting in the backseat of Chris' parked patrol
car as Chris turns around in the driver's seat and glares
at him.

                    NARRARATOR (V.O.)
          Why had he mentioned Chris Simone's
          parents?

EXT. GRASSY HILLTOP - DAY (FLASHBACK)

Chris' mother and father embraced together, expressions at
once serene and at peace, upon a hilltop overlooking a
valley carpeted with a myriad of beautiful flowers.

EXT. CITY STREET - DAY

Tom Burke walks on the sidewalk, unassisted, no more
walking stick or aviator glasses, stopping to chat with
shop owners and passersby, smiling and happy as one could
imagine a newly sighted man could possibly be.

                    NARRATOR (V.O.)
          Of course, what of the one inexplicably
          true miracle: Tom Burke's restored
          eyesight?

EXT. ST. MICHAEL'S CHURCH - CHRISTMAS NIGHT (FLASHBACK)

Jedidiah, returning to the crèche from the scene of the
fire, encounters Tom Burke, stops for a moment and touches
Tom's face. A gleam of light seems to pass between them. As
Tom removes his aviator shades and begins to stare
mesmerized at the aura of the streetlight filled with
falling snow, Jedidiah moves toward the crèche once more.

                    NARRATOR (V.O.)
          In his heart, Chris Simone believed
          the answers rested amongst the crèche
          nativity scene. There were times when
          his logic would counter that it was too
          fantastic to imagine that wooden figures,
          even blessed ones from the Holy Land,
          could influence the lives of mortal men.

          More than anything, Chris simply wished
          to see Jedidiah once more.

          Yet, for the rest of his days it would
          remain his privilege to know the full
          bounty of true faith: Miracles, including
          the magic of Christmas are real as the
          sunrise and sunset, the moon and stars,
          real as the ever-lasting power of an
          undying love.

Jedidiah stops at the entrance of the crèche, looks around for an extended moment, visibly enjoying what he sees, then turns and disappears inside, just as Chris Simone approaches Tom Burke staring at the streetlight and its golden aura filled with falling snow.

Graphics displayed:

Dedicated to the life and memory of Captain Gary D'Esposito of the Ocean Township Police Department, Monmouth County, New Jersey, years of service 1979 – 2006, the truest of gentlemen and a Blue Knight to the core.

FADE OUT

THE END